ARGUILLE MacGREGOR
Domesticated

THE CIRCLE OF LIFE

Arguille MacGregor

Word Art Publishing
9350 Wilshire Blvd
Suite 203, Beverly Hills, CA 90212
www.wordartpublishing.com
Phone: 1 (888) 614 - 1370

Published by Word Art Publishing

ISBN: Paperback   978-1-955070-45-4
        Hardback   978-1-955070-47-8
        Ebook   978-1-955070-46-1

DEDICATION

This book is dedicated to the family members who supported the Author and ignored his cranky disposition through the drafting days, weeks and months to completion. These include his wife, Martha Elena Ceballos Malkum Hern, and five daughters in chronological order of arrival:, Shanna Hern Veale (#1), Lucinda Hern Burnham (#dos), Roberta Hern Sturm (#3), Kara Lee Hern Branson (#4) and Ana Milagros Hern (#5). Thank you ladies for your tenacity and grit. GP

Table of Contents

PREFACE

THE LIFE OF Arguille had developed into an absolute yearning to travel and experience different cultures, locations and determine the elements of his own circle of life. To quench that yearning the opportunities to explore life dynamics presented themselves. In his years of international travel many passengers he conversed with suggested to him he should write a book of his diverse adventures. Either through divine providence or Drake equation probability or pure luck he traversed the continental United States and decided to construct a second book. (1) The 400 trillion to one probability of being born proclaimed by the Drake equation whetted the appetite to understand the uniqueness of the individual and the circle of life they follow. From a handful of cosmic dust to humans fragility at birth they are all extremely special, unique and fortunate to exist. The isolated locations he traveled exhibited tall mountains and narrow valleys, The various locations leant themselves to isolated growth and development. It became obvious to him early on that the various remote locations developed their own microcosms of language, industry, religion, personal relationships, and family. They were completely unique, distinct and beckoned for discovery and sampling. A cordial greeting in one valley such as, "How many children do you have," to the adjacent valley," How many young'uns you got". A true dichotomy as a minimum and both acceptable depending on location and history of the respective conversant.

This was his second attempt to share with the reader a sampling of his life and the many individuals and places Providence had allowed him to sample and enjoy.

He was a believer in the divinely guided events in life and have personal multiple examples to support that belief and make for an entertaining fun read.

Author

INTRODUCTION

ARGUILLE DESIRED TO experience different adventures in the US early on in his young life to compliment his international traveling experiences. He had learned much on time spent with different cultures and locations including similarities between different and distant lands. The inherent differences in us all. He had observed the many unique microcosms that developed and existed at different isolated locations. He looked forward to discovering the different locations and the internal actions in each. His heritage had developed from two sources. One was from the Hern paternal side that arrived on a vessel in New York harbor in 1860. The maternal side arrived in Tennessee in a covered wagon in 1890. Thus the spirit for adventure was innate in the respective lineage DNA

The Drake Equation

where:

$$N = R * f_p * n_e * f_l * f_i * f_c * L$$

N = The number of broadcasting civilizations.

R = Average rate of formation of suitable stars (stars/year) in the Milky Way galaxy

f_p = Fraction of stars that form planets

n_e = Average number of habitable planets per star

f_l = Fraction of habitable planets (n_e) where life emerges

f_i = Fraction of habitable planets with life where intelligent evolves

f_c = Fraction of planets with intelligent life capable of interstellar communication

L = Years a civilization remains detectable

ARGUILLE HAD EXPERIENCED many different cultures during his global adventures and was eager to expand to his domestic U.S. culture knowledge. The travel to China, meeting the South American gorgeous love of his life, near miss on a communist guerilla kidnapping and observation of a Brazilian bank robbery were exciting events that whetted by his appetite for future exciting life episodes. The chance to live with his cultural background held great potential for new episodes of knowledge and adventure.

This thought led to Arguille questioning his own existence and destiny. The understanding of the Drake equation that predicts the probability of an individual being born from cosmic dust at 400 trillion to 1. This amazed him and identified with Common logic. As a leaf is born, grows, lives and finally falls to earth and restarts the process, so does human life. This expands the diversity of the human species and begs for investigation into the Providence validation of The Circle of Life, it's humbling understanding, fragility of and uniqueness.

BISCUITS AND GRAVY

AS THE COMPANY engineer civil engineer named Billy Joe known to Arguille invited him to travel to the remote regions of southern West Virginia. Arguille being a Civil Engineer also a common interest in the local environment would be of interest to them both. The areas were sparsely populated and required a physical walk through about once a year to observe any illegal activity such as moon shining, marihuana cultivivation or other activities. These remote areas were also ideal for digging ginseng root for sale. Previous value for the medicinal plant was $1000 per pound which was a motivational inducement for trespassers to extract the plant illegally. Thus Billy Joe had his usual schedule for Wyoming and McDowell Counties and preferred someone to accompany him on the journey.

Arguille accepted Billy Joe's invitation with the one requirement in the snake proof lower lagans be warn. Copper head and rattle snakes were plentiful in the thick under brush. These lagans were hard plastic that were impervious to the sharp fangs of any reptiles that were nearby. These devices were worn from just below the knee to the top of the foot. Billy Joe was happy to see Arguille had made the necessary purchase and set their travel day for the next Thursday. There was no cell phone service in the area they would be traveling as a pair as it was a necessary safety precaution as a minimum.

Thursday arrived and Arguille met his friend at 4:30 am as the road travel time to arrive at the area was two hours. While traveling to the site entrance area the sun was rising and revealing to Arguille the brilliant coloring of the fall foliage. Like the slow rising of a stage curtain in inverse from top of tree to bottom the brilliance increasing from the red, yellow and orange of the hardwood trees indigenous to the area. Regardless of the rest of the day the early morning showing was breath taking.

They arrived at the eastern edge of the property, donned their plastic legging's and began traversing the property. The heavy thick underbrush and steep mountain slopes made for difficult walking. The narrow valleys created a terrain that was slow to cover by foot. They both had to cut saplings to steady their walk on the steep slopes. The steep slopes required Arguille and Billy Joe to forge ahead taking few rest stops but realizing a total of 3 snake strikes as they proceeded. The protective leggings had done their duty and no injury sustained.

Noon time arrived and the duo decided to take a lunch break. Billy Joe had his wife pack lunches for the two. A typical back pack lunch consisted of bologna and PB&J sandwiches with fruit and was delicious. Remains from the meal were buried as a fire was risky at that time of year. Refreshed from lunch the two restarted their journey. Their first interesting event after lunch was the surprise of an abandoned moonshine still. This was not totally unexpected but noted on the surveyor's map they carried with them. Three hours later they came across a 1000' square foot marihuana patch that had been recently visited. It was a mature planting and would be harvested in the near future. This could be a dangerous situation as the owners of the crop have been known to carry weapons and resist intruders. The location would be noted and forwarded to law enforcement officials on their return.

They had traveled to the property boundary and the two began their return journey to the vehicle. Realizing they had traveled a much longer distance than they had planned and dark was rapidly approaching. Walking through the heavy underbrush and steep terrain would be hazardous and slow. They had passed a farm house on their day time journey and decided to ask for overnight boarding if the owners would allow. Lights were on in the single level dwelling. A group of 3 dogs and multiple chickens guarded the house from intruders and began alerting the inhabitants to their arrival. The front door opened and a medium sized man stood there with a double barrel shotgun in his hands wearing bibbed overalls, a massive red beard and a sleeveless T shirt. Billy Joe immediately announced who they were and who they represented. Billy Joe presented his company identification card to substantiate his identification claim. The tense moment seemed to abate as the man of the house lowered his shotgun. He then asked what they required. Billy Joe proceeded to explain their situation and inquired if they could stay the night. Billy Joe went on to explain the unusual nature of the request but they were in fear of being lost if darkness overcame them.. The owner introduced himself as Bruener Johnson, wife Imogene and two yunguns and a baby on Imogene hip. Told the two he did not have a great deal of room as he had a wife and three children but they could sleep in the adjacent barn. With options limited to one Arguille and Billy Joe accepted the offer of the barn which included an early breakfast.. The farmer politely offered left over fried chicken and green beans as the family had already finished their dinner. The two were quick to accept the gracious offer as they were famished at the late hour. Bruhner Johnson and his wife Imogene provided the strangers dinner and then escorted them to the barn with blankets to sleep on and for cover. They bid the farmer goodnight and settled in for a well deserved slumber. Neither Arguille nor Billy Joe moved the entire night. They sleep as if they were in a coma from their all day trek.

The farm commander, the rooster, announced to the farm inhabitants the new day with a resounding crowing from the barn roof top.. The many animals stirred to start the new day with anticipation of the morning feed.. Arguille and Billy Joe were more than ready for their gastronomic introduction to a backwoods breakfast.. They knocked on the oak door at the entrance to the main building. Entering the kitchen the aroma of fresh coffee, fried pork chops, biscuits squirrel gravy and fried potatoes. Imogene beckoned the guest to be seated. A typical wholesome farmer's breakfast for the hardy non-vegan appetite lay before them.

Imogene was up by 4:30 also preparing breakfast on a gas stove for the family plus two guests. She was somewhat rotund but a lovely lady with pleasant demeanor. A large propane storage tank provided ample fuel storage to service the family requirements. By 5:00 the entire group was up and ready for the start of a new day. Entering the farm house Billy Joe and Arguille gave morning greetings to everyone and they were then directed by Imogene to the family table. The family was already seated. Bubba, Robert, Susan, and baby David on Imogene's hip as she walked around the table. The room was filled with the aroma of biscuits, fried pork chops, squirrel gravy, fried potatoes and coffee which stirred the digestive process. This initiated the rumbling of the stomach juices that only magnified the hunger sensation for the two famished travelers. The remote location of the family dwelling prohibited the advent of a Vegan diet which had not been introduced in the remote area. The menu focused on a hard working farmer. and the associated calorie requirements The usual condiments of honey and apple preserves were available. Bruhner asked for everyone to bow their heads and said a morning blessing of thanks for the bounty they were about to receive. Bruhner spoke in a strong base voice that softened as the prayer proceeded. Arguille found it difficult to hear and had to open one eye to see if Bruhner was still proceeding with the prayer, He was pleased to see others around the home-made table also had one eye open to observe the completion of the breakfast prayer. A semi audible *Amen* was emitted that signaled the end of the thank you and the beginning of the splendid breakfast before the group..

Little conversation was conducted at the outset of breakfast. With a voracious appetite Arguille was greatly enjoying the delicious gravy and biscuits, fried potatoes, chops and coffee to the point a second serving was in order. Arguille had taken care to utilize his biscuit morsels to collect all remaining gravy on his plate. This was a typical menu for a hard working farmer. Imogene circled the table supplying second fills. Arguille was totally enjoying the biscuits topped with gravy. As Imogene passed, Arguille requested milk for his coffee. Imogene stopped next to Arguille, lifted her blouse exposing an ample breast from under her garment and with one hand discharged an appropriate amount of breast milk into his cup. Arguille was visibly astonished at the source of the milk, the size of the breast, accuracy of the delivery and was speechless. Imogene noticing the stark expression commented to Arguille, "I do not know what you are shocked about, from what do you think I made the gravy?"

Not being accustomed to the culture and localized cuisine of the isolated mountain inhabitants Arguille had a difficult time not returning his *delicious* biscuits and gravy back to its point of origin plate. He was certain he had turned pale in front of his host. He graciously declined the additional gravy. Imogene and Bruhner were not offended as they knew they were dealing with city dwellers unaccustomed to the culture of the back woods farmer. Arguille and Billy Joe finished their breakfast, except for the gravy, raised themselves from the table and excused themselves to depart. Billy Joe offered Bruhner twenty dollars for the meal. Bruhner declined the money, thanked Billy Joe and told him they were considered guest and accepting the money would be an insult. Billy Joe was distracted with visions of the beautiful breast he had just seen.

The two adventuring engineers set off to return to their vehicle with breakfast memories they would never forget.

The Condom
and The Pencil

ARGUILLE HAD BEEN working for three lackluster and mundane years in a support functions in the construction and material handling industries. Various positions in the north and miwest U.S. were his temporary residences. He missed the excitement, travel, and friends he had grown to cherish during these international adventures. Thanks to electronic mail he had been able to keep in touch with his many global lists of friends. This led to an invitation from Ian Beckman, a long time friend to visit him down under in Sydney. This was unexpected offer that caught Arguille off guard. He knew he had several weeks of vacation and the timing of the request was excellent. His mother had a stroke in the previous month and he could not afford to place her in a nursing home for her care during his absence. He apologized to Ian and told him the situation. Ian understood but told Arguille the invitation was open ended. Come and visit any time he could find resource mate.

Life drugged on for Arguille with little excitement or adventure. Arguille returned to his hoo hum life. Three weeks later he stopped by his favorite all night market and purchased his usual five play lottery ticket. to be drawn in three days. The ticket was placed in the glove compartment and forgotten. The six day a week twelve hour work days absorbed his time with resting and reverence on Sunday. Arguille was not a very religious person but did believe in a supreme being and divinely guided destiny. With the care of his ill mother his weeks were consumed.

The situation with his ill mother took any spare time that was available. Although demanding, Arguille enjoyed the time he had with her. Her stroke had left her paralyzed in her left side and she was slowly regaining the use of her left arm and leg. Not bad for a lady of 70 years. This limited him from any relationships which he regretted

Two weeks later Arguille had finished work and was enroute to his mother's home. Searching for a pack of chewing gum in his pickup truck glove compartment he came across the lottery ticket he had previously purchased. As the market was on his rout he decided to stop and purchase a grilled Rueben sandwich and check his lottery ticket. He stopped and entered the market. As he walked in, he greeted the owner, Alex, and ordered his grilled Rueben sandwich. While waiting for his gastronomic delight he pulled the ticket from his pocket. He looked for the winning numbers that were always posted for the last four weeks beside the market register. Arguille looked down the register side until he came to the date of his ticket certain this was a waste of time. He began reading the numbers off to see if there was a match hoping against hope. He started: 06-06, 08-08, 19-19, 65-65, Arguille began to become nervous, 10-10, 20-20, and special number 04-04. All the numbers matched!! Arguille had just won the $20M West Virginia Lottery. Containing his excitement, he double checked the numbers four times and promised the Manager $5000 to keep his silence. The numbers were confirmed.

Arguille asked the store manager to meet him outside. Once outside he swore the manager to secrecy until he could contact his lawyer and accountant. The manager agreed and the two parted company until some final arrangements could be made.

After the conversations with lawyers and accountants Arguille had a solid plan for his life. His first task was to schedule proper care for his invalid mother. His research led him to the Hill Valley Rest Home that was only a 2 hour drive away and his mother could reside there with 24/7 care.

The second task was to secure his assets. Arguille decided to take a onetime payout that after taxes came to $5.4M. This allowed him to pay off a $120,000 home mortgage and $10.000 in credit card debt. The balance was put in secure bonds and treasury notes.

He also had preparations to make before his journey to Australia he could now afford. His friend Ian had developed a desire for US whiskey. With this in mind the purchase of two quarts of Jack Daniels and one of Knob Creek whisky were priorities. Passport and Australian VISA were in place and all else were accounted for. A flight from Pittsburg to L.A. to Sydney was scheduled and reserved. First class tickets would cost a fortune. With a $5.4 million cash out winning ticket he felt he could now afford first class travel but settled for business class, a difference of $4000. Even though a new millionaire he was tied to his frugal beginnings.

Arguille arrived in Sydney after a 13 hour flight from LA. Even though the Aussie attendants were very accommodating and pleasant, the long flight had taken its physical toll. Ian was there in Sydney to pick him up. They were both happy to see each other as good friends would do. They retrieved Ian's car from the garage and proceeded in the direction of Ian's beach house. This took them over the Sydney Harbor Bridge and in sight of the world famous

Opera House. Arguille always enjoyed taking this picturesque route. He had the pleasure of being in Sydney Harbor bridge on New Year 's Day previously and was amazed by the Harbor fire works.

It was 11:00 in the morning when they arrived at the apartment. In typical Aussie style the two mates consumed several pints of stout and reflect about their many past adventures. Arguille being exhausted from the trip excuses himself and retired for a short deserved nap.

Awakening at 4:00, Arguille left his room and found Ian on the balcony drinking coffee. He told Arguille he had made dinner plans with their friend Gaeme. An acquaintance of many years and an avid consumer of Aussie beer he defined the Aussie persona. He had a very strong Scottish brogue that took some time to understand. Graeme did have one unique trait in that once inebriated he would shed his clothes and sleep in the nude. Not being of the gay persuasion this unique trait was not understood but accepted by the two other members of the group.

Gaeme arrived at the apartment at 6:00 and after one Guinness stout each and introductory conversation of the threesome left for the restaurant. The dining establishment Ian had chosen was a seafood specialty shop that was well known in the area for the seafood quality. Knowing their collective propensity for alcohol they had decided to travel by taxi to their destination. Arriving at the large open air structure Ian had reserved a table at an open window and within hearing distance of the bar.

Commencing the evening with multiple draft beers samplings the evening was off to a grand start. After the first hour the three mates all ordered the grilled seafood sampler. Ample portions of oysters on the half shell, mudbugs, shrimp, scallops, calamari and of course chips. The seafood was fresh and succulent. An ample feast for sure.

The evening progressed with the only difference being Gaeme changed from stout to bourbon. They continued to party with the patrons and two hours later decided it was time to return to the apartment. Sydney was alive at this late hour and showed no indication of slowing. Gaeme was having some trouble walking so Arguille and Ian assisted on each side of Gaeme. Until they were at the apartment and deposited their almost conscious mate on the couch with blanket cover. The two went into the kitchen, poured a glass full of Port and talked sometime about where their lives had taken them. Having exhausted their life review they proceeded to prepare to sleep. Passing through the living room they observed where Gaeme had removed his clothes and was fast asleep, covered and face to the back of the couch.

Ian not being one to pass an opportunity told Arguille he had an idea. His idea was to take a condom, a pencil and place the condom in Gaeme's rectum while he slept. Let him wake in the morning and not mention the condom. Tell Gaeme a van load of men he had met at the restaurant had dropped him off at the apartment. Arguille at first reluctant to perform the deed but as his intestinal fortitude returned he became more interested in the exercise. Ian went into the bathroom and returned with two condoms.

Gaeme had totally succumbed to the effects of adding bourbon to stout.(termed a "boiler maker" in the U S). Ian turned to Arguille and asked him to open the condom pack, remove one, and put the pencil in the condom. Arguille gave the prepared party favor to Ian which Ian took with a slight smile on his face. Ian slowly placed the pencil with condom cover in Gaeme's anus. Once through the rectum the full length of the #2H writing tool. Gaeme did not realize the act was taking place and numb to the actions. Ian slowly removed the #2H pencil without Gaeme's knowledge and left the condom in place. The deed was complete and the stage was set.

Early the next morning Gaeme had gotten up before Arguille and Ian. Not knowing if Gaeme would mention any reference to the in place condom they waited for any acknowledgement of its existence. Nothing was mentioned. Gaeme asked how he had gotten home the previous night and Ian responded a van load of mates dropped him at the front gate. Gaeme did not question the explanation but looked troubled. Ian and Arguille said nothing but departed to spend the next 2 weeks traveling to New Zealand, Bonsai Beach, Carnavon Gorge, crocodile zoos, dinners on a stern wheeler in Brisbane and other Aussie adventures. It was a full two weeks of travel and sampling the Aussie culture.

At the end of his two week agenda the time arrived for Arguille to return to the U.S. The night before his departure the three had one last visit to the local pub with chilled beer dispenser valve. Two hours into the final evening the two condom perpetrators told Gaeme about the condom insertion they had actioned on their unconscious friend. They went on to explain the van load of men that dropped him off were fictitious. Gaeme was totally shocked and livid at the episode. He screamed and went into a tirade at his two partners. He had not been able to look his wife or family in the face for the entire two week period. Gaeme was so upset he was trembling with anger Ian and Arguille were in convulsions with laughter. Soon as the surprise abated the atmosphere settled to one of having a go by two mates and three mates having a good laugh. Gaeme was impressed with the skill the act had been completed. He also ceased the act of going to bed with no clothes.

Understanding The Alligator Pit

ARGUILLE HAD A first working management position that included dealing with union worker complaints or Grievances. This was all a new experience and transition from a technical focus to one encompassing an HR arena. The procedure had 4 Steps or levels. Step 1 was designed to take place between the worker and the immediate supervisor. Step 1 settlement set no precedent that could be referred to in other Steps or Grievances. This presented Arguille with latitude in negotiations he would not recognize until later in his position. Step 2 took place between union representatives operation management. (Step 2 through 4 were precedent setting and could be referred to in future proceedings). Step 3 was negotiated between senior management and senior union officials. If no agreement, could be achieved in step 3 an independent third party was contracted to arrive at a final binding resolution in Step 4 the final binding arbitration step. This process was developed to eliminate work stoppages as an avenue for negotiations to maintain production and wages.

The first facility he was assigned had a bad reputation for animosity between management and workers. His first experience in this process was a Step 3 meeting with the parties at his new assignment. He was announced as an observer in the process meeting. As he walked into the meeting room he could sense the tension. Each entity was positioned on opposing sides of a rectangular table. A us versus them scenario No one was speaking. The attendees seemed so polarized as an undernourished alligator pit waiting for the daily feed. That gave a close approximation of the tension in the atmosphere.

The issue at hand was a worker that had come to work intoxicated. An automatic discharge event.. The family of 5 living with his father that had lost both legs to diabetes and labored breathing from the industry scourge of pneumoconiosis (black lung). The two sides started the meeting by screaming and yelling across the table with ample use of over utilized four letter words. Arguille had his first lesson in how not to conduct a Grievance meeting. The ultimate ending was the worker was the discharge of the worker. This automatically elevated the process to arbitration or Step 4. Further polarized the parties. The company was more concerned about who won or lost the Grievance versus solving the fundamental problem. The workers defended the individual right or wrong.

Arguille gained insight into the matrix of worker and management communications and realized if he could keep his labor relation issues at the Step 1 level it might reduce tension and cost. Step 1 set no precedent and excluded upper management he could potentially improve relations and eventually facility performance. His first opportunity presented itself when a married worker presented a female employee with a pornographic magazine during work time. This could have developed into a major crisis if not addressed immediately. Arguille knew if Human Resources staff were involved the result would be one of animosity and frustration for all parties. He instead drafted a resignation letter for the worker involved and left the date blank. He then called in the worker that had given the pornographic article to his office and confronted him with the situation. He then told the worker he could discharge him immediately. The only way to avoid this was to sign the document he had drafted and with any future issue Arguille would fill in the date and also mail his wife the document copy and explain its source. The worker reluctantly agreed to the program. Arguille then revealed the program to the female employee and received her approval of the program. He showed her the signed resignation document from the worker. She also signed a document she had agreed to the program and required no further action. Situation resolved and HR not involved. Arguille gained respect of the workforce and expanded on this. He also placed an oval meeting table in the conference room to eliminate the us versus them atmosphere in future Human Resource meetings by not using a rectangular table.

THE LOTTERY

ARGUILLE WAS EARLY to his employment on a Wednesday which was not unusual for his active life style. Early arrival gave him time to meet and greet with the crew and supervisors. The standard jokes and friendly harassments took place before start time arrived.

The state lottery was a standard focal point of most workers interest that day as the six numbers and lottery draw number took place at twelve noon. This took place during the time the workers were having lunch in the climate controlled bathhouse. No one in the 1200-man crew had ever won any of the amounts from the winning numbers but were regulars for ticket purchase in anticipation of becoming rich overnight.

The operation was located in the remote area of Eastern Kentucky. Most of the support facilities were conducted by local contractors. One such task was the daily cleaning of the hourly worker bathhouse. The person assigned to this daily task was John Broody, a man of substantial ego and vocal tenacity. Frankie, an accomplished welder with capacity for humor, was walking through the employee parking lot when he noticed John's parked car. A rectangular piece of paper was a purchased and valid lottery ticket was placed on the dash of John's car The current winning six numbers and Power Ball would be drawn this morning. Frankie retrieved a pen from his jacket and recorded the numbers John had on his ticket and made certain no one was watching his actions.

The workers donned their protective clothing in advance of start time and exited the bathhouse. John could now begin his duties which included the use of a wet mop over the large tile floor. This work took approximately 4 hours to complete which carried into lunch time. As the workers filed into the bathhouse for their usual thirty minute lunch break. Arguille also entered the room and positioned himself close to John and Frankie but visible to the rest of the crew. The lunch break had been proceeding for ten minutes when Frankie decided to pull his list of John's lottery ticket numbers. John had entered the lunch room and with mops in hand sat four seats from Frankie. Frankie began, "hey fellas, I was on the internet and received today's lottery numbers and here they are, 4-16". After the first two numbers Frankie read John had shown little excitement. After the third number John rose from his seat and laid his sandwich down. Walking around the room nervously he waited with timid anticipation as Frankie continued.. He had shown little excitement. John had recorded his numbers so he would have them handy after the draw was conducted. Frankie continued, -22-3-45". John immediately jumped from his seat, threw his mop in the floor and proclaimed, "I have hit five numbers". The final lottery number to call was the bonus number. Frankie then read the final number, "45". John yelled out an excited and loud "YAHOO" that reverberated throughout the bathhouse. I quite this m_______ f______ job I have won the lottery" he screamed. This validated the gullibility of some of the workers and John was a case in point.

It was about two hours later when the news reached John that the lottery win was a hoax. John was livid to an exponential power to say the least. After regaining some level of composure John went on a search for Arguille. The entire facility was laughing over the episode at John's expense which made him monumental angry. John went directly to Arguille and said he planned to resign as he had just won the lottery. Arguille was not aware of the events that led to this statement and congratulated him.

Arguille was versed in human relations and knew what John's reaction would be. He had a feeling of great anger initially and eventually mild jovial acceptance. Based on this understanding Arguille determined it was necessary and timely to take the standard four hour inspection of the ancillary facilities that was required once a week. Distance was his ally. Timing his return to coincide with the end of the shift Arguille arrived at the bathhouse. John spotted Arguille as he approached and ran toward the vehicle. Arguille was at first prepared to defend himself against John but relaxed as John broke into boisterous laughter. "You really pulled one over on me friend, I will be sure to return the favor."

Peace was made with all involved and preparation for showering and returning home were underway. The superintendent had become aware of the hoax but did not let John know he was aware of the joke. He exited his office and walked in the direction of the bathhouse. He stopped just outside the structure and took a position just adjacent to the exit door. Waiting patiently. As John exited the building the superintendent asked, "hey John, do you want your final pay check today or can I just stick it in the mail?" John had forgotten he had earlier resigned before the learning the true circumstance. With shocked expression John immediately began pleading for his job back. To avoid any further stress to John Arguille laughed and told John he had a good laugh and he still had his job but be careful who he resigned to in the future.

John was greatly relieved and never left his lottery ticket on the dash of his car again if discovered.

THE DOWNSIDE OF FLIGHT

ARGUILLE WAS NOW in a position to follow his dreams. Financially secure he had always dreamed of flying. He had dreamed of flying since childhood since his first commercial flight at the age of 10 At the age of 14 he was on a family vacation travelling from Chicago to Miami and was allowed to enter the Captain's cabin. Arguille was over whelmed with all the technology and electronics. Of course, this was some years before the terrorist attack of 9/11 and cabin access was much more relaxed. The 36,000-foot high adventure confirmed the Bucket list item of obtaining his own plan for a Pilot's License.

Arguille befriended a coworker, Johnny, who was a licensed trainer for flight training. Johnny was a medium built bloke with wavy black hair and in his thirties. His profession was an electrician for a local mining and manufacturing operations in southern West Virginia. He too had a passion for flight and owned his own aircraft. Flying in southern West Virginia was a challenge with the narrow valleys and multiple mountain peaks. A lack of concentration could be terminal.

Johnny led Arguille through the written portion of the training. Completing the written portion of the training Arguille was now ready for the hands on portion of the instruction. Johnny had Arguille meet him for lunch at his small farm in the surrounding mountains. This was located 80 miles from Huntington, W.Va. the opiate capital of the U.S.. They met there and Johnny had a delicious smoked pork tenderloin roast ready for their culinary retreat. Johnny housed his personal single engine Cessna at this location. No defined runway existed but a level grassy expanse was adequate to allow a take off and flight initiation. As a first time visitor Johnny took Arguille on a short tour. Johnny had done well as a electrical contractor. He owned a 200 acre tract of mountainous terrain with a flat mountain top conducive to receiving small aircraft. There was also a medium sized hangar that would accommodate the single plane that Johnny possessed.

As they continued their tour Johnny recanted a recent flight he had taken to Florida. A friend had contacted him to transport the remains of a friend that had passed. All had gone well on the trip until the return trip when Johnny was climbing for altitude. As the cabin lost pressure the remains began to lose air to equalize with the reduced pressure in the cabin. The remains began making sounds that would probably resemble a serious demonic possession. He waited for the casket to open but to Johnny's relief it did not happen. Johnny stated he was never as happy before for a flight to end. He never repeated this type of exercise again. Johnny told Arguille he was available tomorrow to take Arguille on his first flight. Arguille. With no hesitation Arguille instantaneously agreed.

The following weeks Johnny instructed his new student on the finer points of flying. The rugged terrain of South East W.Va. required total focus and concentration to avoid a Ritchie Valens final type event. After eight weeks of training Johnny told Arguille he was ready for his first solo flight after the weeks of training Johnny had given him. It was all straight forward. The scary part for Arguille was the stall that always gave Arguille a puckered rearend.

The next Saturday was the planned launch day for the solo exam. Arguille was both excited and apprehensive at the same time.

Saturday arrived and Arguille arrived early for his solo flight. The weather was blue sky and clear for a mid August. The flight plan was to travel to Huntington and on to Lexington Ky. The forecast was similar weather for the entire day. Arguille did his preflight checks and was ready. Arguille started the single and after a ten minute warm up with wing flaps extended he accelerated the engine for take off. The plane advanced effortlessly and was airborne in a short distance. Arguille was elated and airborn.

The return trip was uneventful and pleasant. Arguille recognized the mountain of Johnny's farm. He banked the plane to the left to align with the orientation of the grassy runway. Reducing speed and extending the wings Arguille piloted the Cessna to the hangar and idled the engine. Success!

Arguille was proud of his achievement and passed the news to the entire group of family and friends. Two weeks passed and early on a Wednesday morning Arguille received a phone call. A close Chinese friend and brother pilot, Yu Zhi Gang, called to pass on the bad news. Johnny had been killed when his plane crashed. The accident happened at 2:10 a m. Johnny had struck a high voltage electrical cable that traversed between mountain tops and not visible in the cloudless early night air. After striking the cable plummeting to the ground some 300 feet below.

It was discovered during the investigation 300 pounds of opiates were in the plane. Johnny had been transporting drugs from Florida to his farm in West Virginia for pick up. Arguille was greatly saddened by the loss of a close friend. This explained the early morning flight. The opioid epidemic in the area had claimed another victim.

THE MOUNTAIN MAN

ARGUILLE HAD MADE an association with a local contractor named Mark Kaczmarek. Mark had relatives that had emigrated from Poland during World War II. He was a robust, tall, 300 pound, bushy red haired mountain man that was born and raised in the rugged mountains of southern West Virginia. He presented himself as a descendant of Eric the Red with his massive red hair and beard. Mark had made several business adventures into the mining industry and had reached millionaire status on two occasions only to experience two instances of bankruptcy. He had an affinity for dirt track stock car racing which aided in the arrival to bankruptcy due to adventures lack of success

He had married a young West Virginia girl that was also a red head with a volatile personality. Her name was Billy Gene. She had been raised with a family of a mom, dad, two brothers, and three sisters. Her father name was Arch. He was a very stately man that was the type that commanded respect whenever he walked into a room. He was the manager of a local mining operation. Her mother was an immigrant from Ireland and a recent US Citizen.

An example of Mark's life style appeared one day when Mark approached Arguille at the work place. Arguille greeted Mark while he was talking to two supervisors at the mine site. Mark looked at Arguille and said, "Hey Arguille would you like some moon shine (illegal corn alcohol). I have some at the office". With the knowledge that having alcohol on company property was a federal offense Arguille began shaking his head in the negative and said, "no Mark, we do not have alcohol on the premises do we?" Mark at first made his offer a second time and Arguille again stated for the benefit of the two supervisors in attendance there was no alcohol on the premises. Mark now understood what the correct answer was and responded to Arguille that there was no moonshine on the premises he was referring to another location. The two supervisors departed to return to their assignments. Arguille now confirmed the moonshine existence and said he would come by and get a sample. Arguille had an understanding that one or two half gallons would be in the refrigerator at Mark's on site quonset hut. No other personnel were available so he went directly to the refrigerator. Arguille then opened the refrigerator door and was shocked. There in the refrigerator were twelve one gallon containers of moonshine. Enough moonshine to supply a medium size town for a month. He immediately contacted Mark to meet him away from operations. They met and Arguille instructed Mark on the liability of having this on the property and to get it off site immediately. But Arguille did get one container for himself for his sample.

Arguille knew this was enough contraband to send him to prison for many years if found by federal inspectors. Mark asked him if he could meet him off site for a short conversation. Arguille agreed and they met at a nearby restaurant. Mark said he needed to relate events of the last week to Arguille just to be able to share it with someone he could trust. They met at the restaurant and Mark began.

Mark had a wife that was also red haired and robust. They led a somewhat volatile relationship but on most occasions were civil to each other. At one of the dirt track racing events the wife, Bobby Jean, was in the spectator seats with video camera in hand recording the event. Beer was. served during the event and Mark's wife had conducted her usual consumption while he was driving. It was a fifty lap race and the track was wet from recent rain. This was a stock car event and he was driving his black super charged, V6, 3.4 liter, Grand AM. This made the turns treacherous for the drivers. In a field of twelve Mark found it difficult to maintain clear vision of the track but keep the car under control in the turns giving the conditions. In the thirtieth lap he was entering an elevated turn when to his best ability he lost control and departed the track surface in an airborne trajectory. The car penetrated a block protection wall and was demolished on impact. Mark at first thought he had passed this life but even though the crash was total demolition Mark survived with a bruised arm and other more minor injuries.

Lucky to be alive he pried himself from the totaled vehicle and searched for his wife. Finding her somewhat inebriated he joined her in a substantial amount of liquid refreshment before going to the emergency room for review. Plenty of lumps and bruises but nothing broken or seriously damaged Mark could leave the emergency room.

Returning home Mark was in a certain amount of pain. He took some pain pills and settled in his lounge chair until the pain abated. While seated the thought occurred to watch the video of the car race his wife had taken. Placing the disc in the player Mark located the control and started the player. The video was clear and tracked the race with his wife as the camera man. Mark recognized the lap where he lost control. As the car left the track and crashed into the wall Mark heard his wife exclaim on the recorder, "he wrecked that m___f____ car." This did not make Mark's day. He thought he had come close to death in the mishap and his wife had more concerns for the car condition than Mark.

With his Mountain Man temper running at light speed Mark decided to leave his wife in bed and traveled to one of his many favorite liquid refreshment holes. This is where his buddies and feminine pleasure providers congregated to indulge in adult entertainment. This included but not limited to arm wrestling, pole dancing, lap dancing, just to name a few. Mark entered and greeted the room full of good ole boys, red necks, and hill Billie's all acquaintances of Mark. He ordered a bucket of beers and sat at the nearest friendly table he could find. Opening the first of what was to be many long neck brews he guzzled the first one before lighting his first marijuana roach of the evening.

As the evening wore on into the early morning hours Mark thought he was enjoying himself fully. As closing time approached he was considering going to a local all night establishment. Just before leaving, one of his female acquaintances, Bobby Lee, came to his table and took a seat. Bobby Lee was a stunning brunette with crystal blue eyes and a body that rivaled Helen of Troy. She wore a deep "V" neck tight fit braless sweater, short/short jeans and cowgirl boots. Males in the room enjoyed inviting her to a game of billiards just to watch Bobby Lee bend over the table. She commanded total attention whenever she walked across the room and Mark was no exception as one of the many attendees.

She and Mark had known each other for roughly six years but had never been romantically involved. Bobby Lee being somewhat intoxicated could create the opportunity Mark was looking for. The alcohol and marijuana was a real motivator. He and Bobby Lee began a casual conversation that quickly turned to one of explicit sexual detail. This lead to an invitation for Mark to take Bobby Lee home as she had no roommate. Mark accepted.

Mark had kept a late model Chevrolet pickup truck with a dancing hula girl doll on the dash. The vehicle was in immaculate condition had no console so three could sit comfortably in the front seat. This was not the first priority for this design preference. Bobby Lee got in the passenger side, slid close to Mark. He began to drive and she began to stroke Mark's leg. He gave no protest.

The drive to Bobby Lee's house took thirty minutes along a serpentine mountain road typical of West Virginia terrain. As Mark drove Bobby Lee began chewing on his ear then also messaging his groin area. Mark asked what she was doing and her response was wait and see. Two minutes later she was applying oral sex that Mark was greatly enjoying simultaneously maintaining vehicle control Mark was having difficulty managing the mountainous road path but maintained his route effectively. He had come to realize how experienced Bobby Lee's tongue was and soon reached an explosive climax that caused him to lose car control, He left the road surface and slide to a gravel spreading stop in the local church gravel parking lot. Mark understood when John Denver wrote "Almost Heaven"

Mark was trembling after his very honorable discharge and told Booby Lee how great it had been. She responded and said get me home and I can do even better than that. None the less Mark made record time getting to Bobby Lee's house. She was a divorce' whose previous husband had left her a 3500 square foot ranch home with an indoor massive hot tub. Bobby Lee wasted no time in retrieving a vial of cocaine from her computer desk along with a straw and razor blade. With the aid of the razor blade she formed two straight lines of the drug she collected from the vial. She sniffed one of the lines, patted her nose and turned to Mark. Mark said he had never tried cocaine before but Bobby Lee coaxed him to try the white powder as he would enjoy it. Mark succumbed to the coaxing and for the first time placed a straw in his nostril and inhaled. It did not take long for Mark to feel the effects of the drug. His first response was "WOW". As the white powder took control Mark felt sexually invigorated and along with Bobby Lee disrobing and entering the pool with Mark as he was close behind. Mark also disrobed as he entered the heated human cauldron. He put both arms around Bobby Lee and with the aid of a strong flooring to push from he commenced one of multiple continuous sex acts until sunrise.

Both completely satisfied and exhausted with great effort exited the hot tub. Stepping into waiting towels they booth dried off and put on their clothes. Bobby Lee kissed Mark on the cheek. They both commented on how great the night had been but it was time to part.

Mark dropped Bobby Lee off at the pub where they had met to pick up her car. He drove on toward home knowing his wife was out of town and would not be back until the afternoon. She had tried to reach Mark all night by cell phone and assumed he was having a midnight rendezvous. Mark arrived home and first confirmed his wife was not there. With tired limbs and back he collapsed into his bed. He quickly fell into a blissful deep sleep.

Mark was sleeping soundly until a sharp pain under his chin woke him. He opened his eyes to find his wife with a large pointed Bowie knife pointed under his chin. After arriving home she found Mark in bed in a deep sleep, oblivious to his surroundings. She was looking for revenge for whatever he had committed on the previous night. As Mark awoke he found that the wife had cut a pair of panty hose and secured Mark's wrist and ankles to the four apposing bed post better known as spread eagle. Mark knew his volatile wife had no limits in the action she might take. He was totally immobile. She added force to the knife point just short of cutting him to further get his attention. She then asked Mark, "Are you ever going to f___ around on me again"? Mark being of above average intelligence knew what the correct answer was. In the most apologetic and loving voice he could muster he responded, "no my love" taking caution not to further insert the knife. She continued to keep the knife point to Marks chin for 15 minutes in silence. She then spoke with extreme sincerity, "If you ever screw around on me again you will die a slow and painful death also less your manhood".

After the removal of the knife from his throat and Bobby Jean away from the knife, Mark has been true blue to Bobby Jean and retained with his manhood in tact to this day.

Arguille told Mark how lucky he was and that his story was safe with him even though Arguille was totally envious.

Sisters

ARGUILLE HAD BEEN blessed with two older sisters to contend with which he seldom conversed until they reached the teen years. Not much in common until they reached life beyond puberty. Typical teenage ladies with above average intelligence, looks and charm. Their father and mother had established a home that was quite remote. The motive for this was to keep a healthy distance from teenage suitors and easy observation of the sisters actions, Onlee and Wilda were two opposites. Onlee with a large ego and the Wilda being shy and reserved.

The MacGregor family had their own sense of humor that was spontaneous and pointed. The evening meal was a tradition that required total family attendance. One night at the evening dinner table the entire family was gathered per the usual custom. The father had a favorite treat of putting apple sauce on buttered bread. Onlee being in close proximity to her father watching him intently with concentrated focus on his apple sauce treat. As Robert raised the savory morsel to his lips, Onlee slapped the back of his hand.

The rest of the attendees at the table gasped in disbelief. Retrieving his hand Robert had apple sauce dripping from his eyebrows, nose and chin. He was a brawny fellow supported by a 6'4" frame. He was stern but had a loving family attitude. He turned slowly turned to Onlee direction and as jokingly said, "Onlee, I will skin you". The entire table erupted in laughter.

Arguille was no stranger to tenacity and adventure, Having a flat tire one night not far from the family residence Arguille needed help with the repair. It was a dark night with no harvest moon to guide the way on his trek home. Starting on the single lane road he was guided on his way by the tall pine and oak trees that lined the sides of the road. In the distance he could discern the outline of a vehicle with no lights. He continued to walk the trail home and as he drew closer recognizes the vehicle as that of Wilda's partner. Once beside the oversized Mercedes Arguille realized the car was oscillating left to right similar to an unbalanced clothes washing machine. The inside of the windows were covered by the steamy moisture generated by the inside activities and blocked any visibility of the physical exercise taking place. The rhythmic moans of ecstasy that emanated from inside gave way to the process that was taking place. One voice Arguille recognized immediately as that of Wilda. Wilda and partner were having a horizontal interlude and oblivious to Arguille's presence. Not wanting to interrupt the in progress flight to ecstacy, Arguille walked softly past the passion party taking place. Wilda was validating the MacGregor pedigree as a fantastic lover and earned the title of "Little Egypt" from her college friends as her escapades and her actions correlated to the song lyrics

Not to spoil the moment Arguille walked quietly around the car but could not pass the opportunity to interrupt the action. With a loud clearing of his throat the oscillating car motion immediately halted. Arguille had succeeded in scaring the wits out of his older sister and partner. Content he ad achieved this goal he continued his journey home.

Wilda was the more reserved of the two amiga's with Onlee being the eldest. Onlee sported flaming red hair supposedly indicating a descendant of Eric the Red. This was a natural draw for the opposite sex and she had many suitors. The only issue was she was in great fear of the host of pursuers. She confided her emotions in a diary as her closest confident. The name she confided to was "Dear Gidgett". This was her most dear repository of heated inner thoughts and desires she could only share with a unquestionable trusting friend.

One day Arguille was walking past Onlee's vacant room and noticed her diary resting on her night stand open and unsecured. Seizing on the grand opportunity presented Arguille immediately began reading the sacred and Holy document to it's completion. He then exited the sister's lair with Arguille escaped undetected.

As the evening arrived it was time for the family gathering the time arrived for the evening meal, All became seated and began passing the individual servings of fried chicken, mashed potatoes/gravy, green beans and corn bread. After each person had their third portion Arguille raised his head, looked at Onlee and stated,"I know who you address your diary to".

Onlee knew she had left the diary in her room but was unsure if she had locked it. She responded with a half and half statement, "you do not". Arguille responded,"Dear Gidgett"! Onlee was totally stunned. Her face turned a brilliant crimson red which validated Arguilles response. Wilda waited as Onlee left the room in tears then turned to Arguille and asked,"any good stuff you can tell me"?

Arguille retained what he had read but did not share his knowledge with Wilda. He did retain life long leverage over Onlee.

GONE FISHUN

THE FATHER OF Arguille, Robert, had always pushed the envelope of Arguille's education and experience in science and life. An element of this was on two different occasions he took Arguille on Canadian Fly-In fishing trips in then remote areas of Ontario, Canada. They would drive 1500 miles to where the road terminated at Red Lake, Ontario. A charter float plane to an isolated lake and spend an entire week with no smart phones, televisions, cars, PC-'s or people. With these uninhabited serene location the walleye and northern pike fishing was aggressive, awesome and productive. Arguille fell in love with all the elements of the journey.

Arguille's father also had favorite sayings for the children whenever they displeased him. They were "ignorant dope" and "knuckle head". Neither having precedence um fishing boat,over the other but having equal impact depending on the severity of the offense. This was quite useful on one particular fishing trip. Arguille was in the front of the aluminum fishing boat, Robert was in the middle, and the guide was at the back controlling the motor and our path.

Three hours into the morning the fishermen had taken advantage of the accommodating walleye and had stringerd 8 trophies. As Robert was in the middle of the boat he was in command and control of the stringer that held our trophies. Arguille hooked the next fish and reeled it to the side of the boat. In anticipation Robert unlatched the stringer Rrobert took the fish and m the boat. Robert then unlatched the bale for the next fish. Arguille unhooked the new catch and turned to Robert and passed the fish. Robert took the fish, hooked on the bale and dropped the stringer in the water. The stringer fioated away, and floated away and floated away. Robert had forgotten to connect the stringer to the boat!! Stunned silence settled over the group. Finally Arguille turned to Robert and sheepesly said, "is this an ignorant dope or knuckle head" moment?

Life continued for Arguille to include a wife and five daughters. Trapped in the mundane life of parenting, Arguille yearned for the adventure of the Canadian wilderness. The daughters were of an age where they could accommodate the hazards of the wilderness but may not appreciate the solitude and separation from their friends and ear lobe conjoined cell phones.

Arguille explained over the family dinner his plan for the adventure for them all to travel to Canada for a fishing trip. First complaint from the daughters was missing their friends. Arguille assured them they would be there waiting when they returned home. He also mentioned that since the travel date was three weeks away the planning needed to start immediately.

Having made the trip on two previous occasions Arguille knew the limitations for baggage allowed on the De Havilland Otter float plane with a single rotary piston engine.. These aircraft were extremely dependable but left passenger with deafened ears. As no roads existed in the remote area it was only accessible by air from Red Lake. Provisions for six days, warm clothing, bedding, fishing tackle and coolers for the frozen packed foods were the required complement. One week before the trip Arguille reviewed with each individual what had been packed. The review dictated a reduction in weight by 50 percent as a maximum was in place by the operator. Needless to say the four daughters protested the reduction in clothing they could take but Arguille ruled.

Departure day arrived and with a mom, dad and licensed teenage daughter available the plan was to drive continuously for the 1500 mile trip. Starting in West Virginia in early June the only concern was the winter ice had not left the lake we were to depart from but undeterred we left excited.

After two days of around the clock van travel, crossing the international Canadian border, and fifteen video movies for family crowd control they arrived at their destination of Red Lake, Ontario, Canada. This was the first trip to Canada for all except Arguille. Everyone departed the van, stretched their legs seeing the beautiful blue water of Red Lake indicating the Lake ice had disappeared and their maiden flight was possible. Excitement filled the air with the scheduled single engine float plane at the harbor dock. Arguille went to the dock office and confirmed their arrival with the owners. Flight for the lake they would be visiting would depart in two hours.

The task of off loading the van, transport and loading the plane was next after a hearty Canadian meal at the local tavern in the Town of Red Lake. The provisions and other materials had to be loaded and securely stored for flight safety. After breakfast and loading it was time to depart. As this was a family operated business there were no pre flight safety review or individual seating. The seats ran parallel to the fuselage of the plane with waist type seat belts. There were minimal if any luxuries, This was by definition of a "bush" plane. No luxuries but necessities only.

The pilot entered the front of the plane and introduced himself to them all. He had previously confirmed the baggage was secure and now gave instructions for the plane to be untethered from the dock. He then turned and started the rotary piston De Havilland engine. They maneuvered to the middle of the harbor, turned and increased the engine revolutions. The plane moved from a slow start to a lifting wake from the water. The engine was loud and to communicate they had to talk loudly above the engine. After an hour and a half of flight time the pilot signaled to the lake below as their destination. Arguille could see a lake of roughly 2 ½ mile diameter with a small wood cabin on one bank. No other structures were visible indicating the area was vacant.

The pilot circled the island which revealed a dock and large rock protruding the water 50 meters from the cabin. They water landed and power floated to the dock and secured the plane to the dock. The girls were all excited and exited the plane in a rush. Grabbing their belongings and the provisions they started the short trek to the cabin. They noticed three Linde aluminum fishing boats secured to the dock which would be their transportation around the lake and platform to attack the fish, Little did they notice the leaches next to the water bank but this would be one of the many experiences in front of them.

The cabin was a wooden structure with four double bunk beds, two burner hot plate stove, gas refrigerator and plumed with gas piping for lighting. Propane tanks were ferried in by plane to support the gas utilities. A wood stove was in the middle of the one room cabin for warmth. The girls wasted no time in climbing into their beds noticing the walls were adorned with the legacy of previous visitors. On the walls were historic records of the previous visitor etchings carved with knives or written with felt tipped pens. The first question of the four young travelers mind was where were the bathroom.. Arguille had the pleasant task of informing the group the toilette was a separate structure with a door and no running water or light. A single seat with a sanded smooth non splintered opening was the only "appliance" available but accompanied with toilet paper and disinfectant aerosol spray. After all belongings and provisions were stored in the cabin a leisurely get acquainted tour was conducted by Arguille. The vivid evergreens, white granite and beautiful water were impressive for all. A bald eagle had landed on the singular large rock protruding from the water consuming the fish remains the previous cabin occupants had left for that purpose. Dinner was created with fried potatoes, fried ham and salad transported from home. Famished as they all were it was a short dinner due to the eagerness to see the Northern Lights. Once outside the cabin and in total darkness the Lights were no disappointment. Long, vertical sheets of lime green translucent light that waved as in a moderate horizontal wind cooled the evening and the sad song of the loons flying overhead in the dark was a slumber opiate.

Sunrise occurred and all were asleep except Arguille. A regular early riser he decided to take a bath on the dock at the lake. A short trek to the dock and with the assistance of a 5-gallon bucket Arguille drenched himself in the bitter cold lake water. Another detriment beside the cold water were the active leaches to avoid.

Returning to the cabin Arguille heard the youngest daughter rise from her bunk and asked "did you go swimming"? He responded, "How else do you think I got this wet"? This response was a physiological trap soon to be realized.

Of course all the women had to use the frontier rest room. Ample use of aerosol disinfectant was applied per derriere to destroy any hidden insects. What seemed to be excessive applications each respective bottom returned refreshed and prepared for the day. Now the time had arrived to disembark for a day of fishing.

The girls were well experienced in the art of fishing. Two were left handed and two were right handed and open faced reels for each were provided including a fifth left hand reel for Arguille. Artificial floating lures were the bait of the day and were designed to float to the surface when not being retrieved. Thus this was the first mishap of the trip. The middle two by age were in their boat and casting around an island. As the third eldest daughter cast she had lightened her grip on the rod and as she cast the entire rig went into the water. Not a total catastrophe but this just happened to be the favorite rig of Arguille. An open face reel and boron rod for a left hander which Arguille and daughter were accustomed.

Hearing the news after pulling alongside Arguilles boat his first impulse was rage but subduing this he turned to the daughters. He then told the daughters no problem he had other rigs but began calling the daughter "Rodney".

Everyone had a productive and exciting day of fishing and the result was a delicious dinner of fresh Canadian walleye. This was the menu but the topic was "Rodney". This new name frustrated the daughter and provided her with a challenge of how to solve this unwanted notoriety.

Early the next morning Arguille notice the two in the "Rodney" boat had left early before anyone else had breakfast. Trusting the intelligence and experience of the two daughters Arguille did not protest and let the two be on their way. The sound of a motor starting was soon heard as the two young fishermen departed. Traveling toward the east in the early morning they were near the location where they had finished fishing the previous day.

The other four members of the group finished breakfast, cleaned the kitchenette, grabbed their gear and headed for a morning of fishing and boating. This being the first morning of fishing the participants had to get accustomed to the aggressiveness of northern pike and walleye just after the spring lake ice had exited. The pike species was known as fresh water barracuda for being extremely fast and possessing rows of razor sharp teeth. They gathered for a late afternoon lunch at the fire pit near the dock. The four started a fire and the Rodney two marched up lastly with a stringer of eight nice fish and the gear they had lost the previous day. Arguille was amazed and curious how they had retrieved the gear from the bottom of the lake. Their early departure allowed them to scan the calm water surface and spotted the wake of the floating lure. Pulling the lure with line attached from the lake the gear was retrieved and the connotation of "Rodney" was erased after presenting the rig to the rightful owner.

Arguille and the wife decided to make it an early afternoon after having caught and released their share of trophy size walleye. Boating across the lake in the fresh Canadian breeze they approached the boating dock. Easing up to the edge of the dock Arguille silenced the boat motor. As soon as the engine noise stopped the terrified screams of two teenage girls broke the silence from the cabin. Arguille knew immediately what had happened.

Arguille had taken his bath using a five gallon bucket at the dock thus avoiding the leaches that thrived at the interface of the lake water and shore land. As long as in the main body of water no leach threat existed. Arguille failed to pass on this small fact of nature as a lesson in life for the daughters. Arguille and the wife entered the cabin and saw two terrified daughters with wooden matches slowly removing leaches from their arms and legs. The teens had returned from fishing and decided to take a swim near the dock. All was fine until they exited the lake by the bank edge when the leaches attacked. Seeing their mother and Arguille at the doorway they asked Arguille, "How did you go swimming in the lake and not get leaches on you"? Arguille responded," I never told you I went in the lake, you assumed I went in the lake.". To say the girls were incensed is an understatement but they learned the lesson of be careful when making assumptions and never trust your father.

Having enjoyed fresh wild fish for the entire week although delicious was getting monotonous for the girls. Absent from a McDonalds or Wendy's was having its pallet effect. Knowing this would develop Arguille had secretly hidden a frozen five-pound prime rib roast in one of the food coolers. As Arguille was an accomplished chef a roasted beef delicacy over an open fire would be in his skill set. The aroma of the roast cooking filled the air and motivated the stomach juices for the entire beef starved troupe. To make this a departure feast including fire roasted potatoes and sautéed mushrooms that were all transported from home.

Arguille and the wife made sure the girls were kept busy outside until the meal was ready. They then covered the cabin dinner table with utensils and food. Called to the table all 5 girls were seated and waiting for the Blessing before beginning. Arguille completed the Blessing, and everyone was seated at the table with a goodly portion of beef, potato, and mushroom gravy on each individual's plate. He then observed an act of human nature he had never seen before, a human feeding frenzy. Not a word was spoken and the room would have been silent except for the moans of beef ecstasy on the part of the teenage carnivores. The roast was devoured rapidly but each morsel was slowly savored. The table was now clear of all food and encircled by 6 well fed fisherman. Now the time was at hand to complete packing for the return flight out tomorrow. The "keeper" fish had been filleted, wrapped and frozen in the propane gas freezer that was supplied with the cabin. All items that had been brought in had to be repacked for transport home. The only addition was all garbage had to be packed for return also. One last visit after dark was taken to observe and stand in awe of the Northern Lights. A good hour was taken by all to observe the soft movement of the lime green display.

A somber ending to a once in a life time family adventure.

Five Daughters/Five Lessons

THE LATER IN life for Arguille with the good Lords guidance saw to it he was blessed with five off spring that happened to be all female. Each daughter about 4 years apart from their nearest sibling. Arguille understood how precious life was as estimated by the Drake equation. The rough approximation indicating the probability of being born starting from cosmic dust to a human birth was approximately 1 in 400 trillion. (restricted to one galaxy). Therefore just being alive was a tremendous gift and should be treated with care, tenderness and amazement...

Arguille was often reminded of the humor response of a father in a similar situation of 5 daughters and no sons, Why no sons?" he asked as he looked into the heavens.? The clouds separated, a bright light appeared and in a deep booming voice the Lord responded, "I send no men where none are needed."

Arguille subscribed to the philosophy that we are all special and unique and with a low probability of being delivered at all. Through Devine intervention starting with cosmic space dust through to birth the probability of each person being born is approximately 400 trillion to 1 per the Drake equation.(1) One individual human female carries 300,000 eggs at puberty. Each egg is with a unique and distinct DNA for each of the 300,000 eggs (2). Thus Arguille was amazed at the of human diversity and existence but had a grasp of how it was achieved.

With all these many offspring he would call them by their respective chronologic number #1 through #5. Number one was a blonde, blue eyed beauty that had the typical dizzy blond syndrome in early life. With five daughters to support the disposable income budget was extremely limited. Therefore the first teenage car was an Isuzu Trooper with 90K miles but in good condition. The color was copper tone and the right front wheel had a constant rattle on each revolution from a loose wheel cover. As Arguille wanted each of the daughters to be able to drive a 4 speed transmission the Trooper was fitted with this type of speed control. For $6000 this was just the correct investment on novice teenage drivers.

#1 was starting her junior year in high school and approached Arguille while he was at home reading the newspaper. As with all young teenagers at this time in life #1 main priority in life was to be able to drive a new car. So she walked in the house one day, dropped the Trooper keys on the table next to Arguille and said, "Dad, I refuse to drive the Trooper any longer and I want a new car"! Now as she was 16 years of age he had learned that as a parent you had to communicate with this age group as young adults and not children and try to outwit them as they were all intelligent and energetic. Arguille paused for a moment and then said, "So you are not drive the Trooper anymore?" The response was verbal and direct "that's right". "And you expect me to buy you a new car, "correct". "Correct" she replied. Arguille continued, "first, I am not buying you a new car, if you maintain a 3.5 GPA for the semester I will consider purchasing a good used car, and with you refusing to drive the Trooper I save on gas, insurance, tires, tag fees and maintenance." I

LOVE YOU"! Arguille asserted. #1 was totally unprepared for this response from her father. She stomped off to her room for fifteen minutes fuming. After which she appeared from her room, walked over and grabbed the keys off the table, left the room in silence, assumed the drivers position in the Trooper and drove off to school.

She did, however connect with the offer of a good used car based on the GPA condition. She maintained the 3.5 and as Christmas approached Arguille realized he was going to have to purchase a car. A good condition vehicle was located with 36,000 miles, sun roof and automatic transmission. This was kept secret from #1. Also prior to Christmas Arguille would purchase local newspaper want ads and search for used cars. He would find one advertisement that read,"100,000 miles, runs good, looks rough, $1000". He would circle the add with a black permanent marker and leave these around the house for #1 to come across. Young adults ages 13 to 18 are totally gullible and easily taken advantage of to ones delight and amusement.

The parents had come across a key chain that resembled a Trooper and was painted as with zebra stripes. Christmas morning they parked the used car outside the house with an oversize red bow on top. The zebra keys were hung on the 16 foot high evergreen Christmas tree. All four daughters came downstairs to see what Santa had brought. All were busy except #1 as she could not locate her gift. She turned to Arguille and asked, "Where is my gift"? He responded for her to look on the tree. #1 turned and scanned the tree and spotted the key set. Lifting the keys off the tree Arguille instructed, 'now go outside". As #1 was 5 feet from the house door Arguille said, "we got a paint job for the Trooper" #1 stopped in her tracks and emitted words he had never heard before. They were English but he was certain they were only used in a red neck pub and not for general conversation. Arguille laughed and told #1 to go outside. She regained her composer, clutched the keys and proceeded out the door. Her first sight was the sun roofed car with large red bow on top. She immediately burst into tears of joy and asked, "Can I drive it now"?

Lesson #1: Teenagers can be totally gullible and objects of great enjoyment between ages13 to 17.

Arguille daughter #er (Chinese for number 2 more pleasant than the biological meaning) was born with a red skin tint. At first thinking she was ill the delivery physician asked if there was Indian blood in her ancestry. The answer was yes as her great grandmother was a 100% Cherokee Indian. This explained the red tint at birth and a natural propensity for the outdoor life. In time she would be a woodsman, State Park Ranger government security guard and a mom of three.

As #er matured into her early teens Arguille watched as she entered into a time period of extreme acne. Large red blotches appeared on her face. This propagated over the entire facial surface. This developed to the point of disfigurement. Arguille was deeply saddened by this knowing the age situation for #er. This appearance created a situation where her classmates avoided her except for two friends with disfigurements of their own and befriended her during this time.

Her mother contacted a local skin specialist and set up an appointment for a review of the condition. The doctor did a complete physical along with blood work. The condition was diagnosed as over active glands for her age of 13. A medication could be administered once a week and get it under control over time. There were side effects that she had to be cognizant of and one of which was deformation of a child if she became pregnant during this time. Not that she was sexually active but the notion of the effects was unsettling.

Over the next three years as time progressed the facial inflammation dissipated but extensive scaring remained. Arguille remained hopeful this condition would correct itself also. The senior prom approached and no bids of a date surfaced. To help motivate the male population Arguille promised to have his 1978 Corvette T-top he owned refurbished. It was currently on jacks and under repair in the family garage. This would be her Cinderella chariot. Soon after she had a date for the Prom. Not sure this was related to the car.

Two weeks before the dance she asked Arguille what color dress she should wear. Arguille had seen the dresses some of the other teenage ladies were wearing. With openings randomly cut in their garments and traced with rhinestones he was not impressed with the less than angelic attire that was the norm. Arguille told #er since she was a brunette a solid black conservative dress would be good. Even though bucking the trend of her peers she complied with his wishes.

Prom night arrived and #er was an excited teenager looking forward to her senior prom. Her dates parents dropped him off and they commandeered the Corvette and off to the Prom they went. Arguille and the mom worried how the event would go hoping all the best for their daughter. Mid night rolled around and #er after dropping off the date pulled into the home driveway. Arguille and mom were waiting in the living room with guarded anticipation of the events of the night. #er walked slowly into the room with the parents expecting the worse. She looked up, stared them in the face and proclaimed, **"I was voted Prom Queen"**! The exuberance gushed from her like thru Old Faithful geyser. Arguille was overjoyed at the happiness his daughter was experiencing for the first time in four years.

Lesson #Er: In strife persistence, tenacity and faith will prevail!!

#3 was the wild child and always happy. Not one for formal attire her clothes seldom matched in color and style until the teen years. A tender heart that was evidenced when her mother was preparing a salad for dinner and made mention of artichoke hearts. #3 asked her what she was doing and she responded, "Opening a jar of artichoke hearts". Huge tears streamed down #3 face and she questioned, "artichoke hearts"? Her mother had to explain to her the anatomy of the "hearts" being vegetable not animal and all was soon well.

Arguille had always been a fan and player of chess. He had acquired a white and brown Gothic set and kept it displayed and ready for action in the family dining room. With chess players six inches in height it was difficult to ignore when entering the room. One day while cleaning the chess set Arguille noticed #3 coming toward him. She stopped and asked if he would teach her how to play. Being eight years of age Arguille assumed she would be all afternoon learning and doubted retention of the various pieces move styles. So he began with the basic board set up, the pond, castle, knight, bishop, queen and finally king. Explaining the respective moves as he went. #3 totally focused on the beginners match.

As expected the first game ended in check mate for dad in 12 moves and several mistakes by the newcomer. Second match begins with #3 first having the white players and first move. A strategic move with pond and knight were impressive. Twenty six moves later it was check mate for dad but somewhat of a struggle. Now on to match three. Arguille had the first move and started by releasing the versatile queen to do battle. Six moves later #3 captured the queen.

Ten moves later #3 had dad in check mate!!! Beaming with pride #3 waited for her congratulatory surrender from dad she received from him, "I refuse to play you again"?

Lesson #3: Intelligence has no age determinate. Never underestimate the competition no matter the age

#4 became 6 years of age as she entered the remote locations of The Peoples Republic of China following her father's work assignments. She was a pleasant child with big heart and. With her childish demur and innocence attracted the attention of most residents. The expat camp was located in Shanxi Province near the town of Peng Shuo. The Expat community contained a total of 35 families with children of all ages. One female child that was 13 years of age and somewhat heavy set was the only camp resident that did not care for #4. She took an immediate dislike to #4 and unknowingly introduced Arguille to his first evidence of "bullying". The Chinese peasants would steal highway covers to sell for scrap. The 13 year old one day spotted an open cover and #4 on her bicycle and proceeded to kick her bicycle into the opening. She was shaken but not seriously injured.

Arguille heard of the incident across the dinner table and realized #4 needed an equalizer to defend herself when everyone else was absent. He retrieved a 33 inch baseball bat and presented it to #4 with the instructions that the next time she was attacked by the 13 year old to use the bat on her for her defense. Four days later Arguille was driving up to the driveway at his home. He came to a sudden stop when the 13 year old ran across in front of his car. Thirty feet behind her came #4 with the bat at the ready if needed. This ended the bullying.

Time passed and #4 returned to the U.S. with her family. As she began her schooling loca she was unfamiliar with protocols in domestic schools having been schooled in China. Schooling in the expat community was a large one room that accommodated grades 1 to 6 in one room and multinational students. Entering a 4th Grade classroom for the first time in the U.S. was daunting at the large number of students and only one class grade. She approached timidly but fit well into the social fabric of the various 4th Grade personalities.

Valentine day rolled around and the day was a Thursday. All four of the girls at that time (#5 had not arrived yet) were in their respective classes. The classroom of #1, now fourteen years old, was quiet but studious. A knock at the door reverberated through the class. Annoyed at the interruption the instructor opened the door. The local flower shop delivery man had a bouquet of flowers addressed to #1. Gushing with embarrassment and excitement all at the same time she accepted the flowers wondering which admirer had sent them.

#ER and #3 received gifts under the same scenario but different gifts. They each received heart shaped boxes of a variety of chocolate candies wondering with great anticipation which suitor had sent them. As all three opened their respective gift cards much to their dismay and surprise the gifts had been sent by a very caring #4.

Lesson #4: Tenacity and warm heart can come in the smallest package.

Arguille had remarried to a Colombian wife in later years. He was 50 years of age, she was 38 and never had children. She had requested of Arguille to have at least one child. Arguille stated that at 50 years of age he was not going to be around forever but agreed to the effort required with that understanding. Several months after the wedding they went together to a physician after not conceiving. The test for Arguille was to deposit a "sample" in a provided sterile container. The container with sample had to be kept warm, sealed and would be transported immediately after "collection" to the laboratory. The means of transportation was the sterile container between the wife's breasts to the lab as a means of maintaining temperature. After all the test were completed they were all assuming Arguille was the issue it was learned to their surprise the wife had some issues. The doctor informed them the possibility of conceiving was low and they should consider adoption in part due to the age of the wife. They thanked the doctor for his review and recommendation but later agreed that adoption was not an option. They decided to leave it in the hands of The Almighty.

Four months later #5 was in the oven and the mom was totally excited. #5 arrived in good health and a bundle at 9 pounds and 3 ounces she arrived on October 8. As time passed she grew rapidly into a beautiful young adult as did the four sisters.

She had a natural attraction with young children. Every where she traveled, China, Australia, Brazil, South Africa and Colombia young children she had never met would come to her for affection.

Lesson #5: They are all special.

THE TARGETED IRISHMAN

ARGUILLE WAS CARRYING the gray colored coffin of a friend of many years. Clarence Green, a devout Irishman at heart, was being laid to rest in the cool green mountains of an spring, West Virginia day. Arguille had met Clarence through a work employee impromptu gathering in a local pub (watering hole) for local residents and wayward passerby's. The name of the establishment was "Babe's" after the owner who was a thirty three year old blond, blue eyed beautiful woman. She was a member of the U.S. Kickboxing team and was well known for her capabilities. Those who had tested those skills paid a brutal price. She answered to the name of Imogene with a nick name of *Babe*.

The surprising portion of the story is Clarence was her husband of ten years her senior. How he maintained without any bruises from this relationship amazed the locals. Clarence and Arguille had worked around each other for some time before their introduction. They immediately struck a friendship. He was a pleasant man but was notorious for his hair trigger temper and massive four letter word vocabulary. Clarence had a job description that he traveled the West Virginia mountains maintaining security fences for the local mining operations. This job was conducted in all seasons and required a rugged individual that Clarence fitted well. Six feet tall and 220 fit pounds described Clarence. A consummate weight lifting enthusiast he was not to be confronted without purpose.

Weekends found Clarence buddies (mates in the down under) and he at Babe's having their weekly reunion and beer fest. The morning passed into afternoon when most had consumed more than their share of brew, The thought crossed their minds of going on a fire arm target practice shoot with their respect fire arms. Each had secured suspended rifles in the back window of their respective pickup trucks. Arguille had a Humvee SUV while three of the group had a collection of Dodge 250 and Ford 250 4wd vehicles. They loaded up with multiple practice rounds for the rifles and ample cases of beer to maintain the fest. The five vehicle caravan traveled the two lane highway asphalt road into Mingo County. This transformed into a dirt mine access road that serpentined into a one lane less than well maintained dirt access route. On the trip they observed wild turkey, deer, black bear, eagles, etc. on the 200 acre reclaimed mine property. On they traveled and entered a dense over grown area of over growth for a short distance. Hardwood and evergreen trees, ferns and various grasses lined the route before them. They forged ahead into this unknown area anticipating the trail ahead. Then as what the Vikings would have envisioned as entering Val Hala (Viking heaven) a bright open expanse of marijuana lay directly before them. The marijuana was a mature crop of six foot tall stalks well maintained. The party crew hastily parked and realized the well kept crop cultivators were probably armed and near by. With rapid execution the traveling targeteers managed to strip three pounds of leaf's from the concealed internal stalks, bagged them and regained their vehicular trek forward motion.

Clarence had collected his own one pound foliage trophy to return with and ample for future use. He and Arguille continued on their quest until they reached a favorite stopping area with thick evergreens, a small trout stream and sandy bank. The crew parked and exited their vehicles. A small fire was ignited and with the metal wire mesh grill they had brought began cooking steaks over an oak wood ash fire. As the steaks cooked the crew removed their rifles from their carrying cases as they did as a practice as they had a custom of target shooting on clear weather weekends. As this was the first clear weekend in three weeks they were eager to retest their marksman skill and reestablish their mountaineer man hood.

The area that was chosen was usually used for local "turkey shoots". These usually held prior to a major holiday such as Thanksgiving. Each traveler retrieved their respective individual weapons to take part in the competition. Clarence was the leader of the group and instructed one of the members to place three targets across the small stream for the first series of firings. The targets were 36 inch white squares with 3 concentric red circles with a center bull's eye. Spaced separately across the stream from where they stood a total distance of 100 yards from each target that were 10 yards apart.

Each member of the entourage took their turn with Clarence being the most accurate of the contestee's. As he had won the first round all retired to consume a freshly grilled steak from the grill and a goodly portion of brew. It was time now for the next round of attempts. Dan, a six foot tall ex marine was next. As he approached the firing location he turned to Clarence and stated that since Clarence had won the last round he should hold the target over his head. Not being one to ignore a challenge Clarence accepted the challenge and went to the area of the targets. He stopped in the area the targets lay. He picked the closest target, held the edges and raised it over his head with the red concentric circles and bulls eye facing the crew. Jim, a team member grasped his bolt action 30 06 and took aim at the elevated target. He took a deep breath, confirmed his grip, checked his sighting, slowly exhaled and fired the gun. The distance did not allow to visibly see where the bullet struck. There was a short pause.Suddenly Clarence collapsed to his knees, continued to fall and lay silent on the ground face down. The group was stunned. After a short pause they then collectively ran to Clarence. They rolled his body over. He had been struck middle of the chest. by the shot. Arguille kneeled and felt for a pulse. No pulse could be located. The crew was devastated by both the loss of a great friend and the overwhelming stupidity of their actions.

Internet access was non existent in the area they were located the same applied for cell phone access. The crew gently loaded Clarence remains into Arguille 's vehicle and started the return trip. As soon as Arguille acquired cell phone service he contacted 911 and informed them of the situation. He told the operator he was taking the body to the clinic in Williamson, the closest medical facility.

As Arguille approached the clinic he realized two patrol cars from the W.Va. State Police were in attendance at the emergency entrance. A physician and 2 attendees were present, Arguille pulled to a stop in front of the emergency entrance. The doctor and attendees opened the car doors. The doctor immediately entered the vehicle and placed his stethoscope to Clarence's chest. The inevitable notice was given. Clarence had passed. The two policemen took the crew into one of the waiting rooms. There they began taking statements from all involved individually.

A detective for the State had arrived and reviewed the information that had been collected and the conclusion of questioning. The detective approached Jim, told him he was under arrest for the third degree manslaughter of Clarence. He then read him his Miranda rights, put him in handcuffs and guided Jim into the police car. The detective told the rest of the crew to not leave the State.

Two days later Imogene, the wife of Clarence approached Arguille if he could be a pall bearer to assist in laying his friend to rest. Clarence having been a true friend and associate Arguille was honored to accommodate the request and agreed. He was now taking an old friend to his final rest which for Arguille was the greatest of honor.

The fire arm practice sessions were no more.

G. W.

ARGUILLE WAS IN the process of establishing a reputation as a facility and industry Human Resource problem solver. He was active in three small operations in Kentucky when his supervisor contacted him about a new expanded position with many challenges This position was to test him had become available. If interested Arguille needed to interview with a mine manager named G. W. in two days. Arguille agreed.

Arguille was aware of G.W. reputation as an Ex Marine that gave inflammatory direction and was intense. He was extremely aggressive to add to the mix and extremely intelligent. He also had a reputation of running from worker desk to worker desk to intimidate staff the staff to perform.

Arguille arrived at site in ample time for his interview. Presenting himself to G.W.'s secretary The secretary notified G.W. Arguille had arrived and he was escorted into the office. On the door leading into the office was the name G. Windelkoski. Entering the office there sat G.W. in his high back chair of austere but massive construction. He was a small man of strong physique. Extremely direct he introduced himself and Arguille the same. He asked Arguille to cover his background which Arguille obliged. In the conversation they touched on mutual acquaintances' and compared notes on their respective experiences. Thirty minutes into the conversation there was a knock at the door. In walked Paul, a fifty year old, medium build man who through stress projected a much older age and spoke with a stutter. This is the man Arguille was to replace. He had a nervous breakdown working for G.W. along with developing the stutter. Labor relations had been an issue at the facility for some time. The 41 employees at the facility had generated 31 grievances while the 330 employees at the mine had generated 4 grievances for the same year. Something was amiss here Arguille sensed.

Paul and Arguille toured the site and returned to the office of G.W. A short review of the tour and questions were conducted. All satisfied Arguille bid farewell and thanked the two men for taking the time to spend with him.

Two days after returning Arguille was informed G.W. had accepted him for the position and Arguille agreed. One week to make arrangements and he was on his way. The first day on the job and Arguille again presented to the secretary. While waiting beside her desk he heard a loud angry voice through G.W. office door say, **"what are you going to do f___ around until you get my blood pressure up"!!** The first thought of Arguille was oh Lord, what had he gotten himself into and where was the closest exit door?

The secretary directed Arguille in the office of G.W. and he proceeded. Turning the knob and entering the office he gave greetings to GW and the two men sitting there, both red faced with embarrassment from the wrath of GW. GW introduced them as James the mine manager and George the chief engineer. GW wished to talk with Arguille in privateon the start of his first day and dismissed the other two attendees. They did not seem saddened to be leaving.

Arguille sat in front of GW while he phoned Paul to come and pick him up at the office. While waiting GW welcomed him and looked forward to their association. Paul entered the room, spoke for a moment then he and Arguille departed for the facility. GW had officially handed the management reins over to Arguille. During the next three weeks Arguille learned the fundamentals of the facility issues. The previous superintendent was having affairs with two of the workers wives, the superintendent Arguille was replacing had personal issues with the crew and the maintenance foremen had construction backgrounds and not a clue on how to maintain a facility which was not performing well and quality had been rejectioable from the client. At this point in time GW calls and invites Arguille and Paul to his office as he had not talked to him since his first day.

Arguille and Paul enter the office of GW and take chairs immediately in front of his desk. GW sits in a roller type desk with a high back that is big for a man of his medium size. He leans back in the chair and looks at Arguille and ask, "Well what do you think of what you have seen over the last 3 weeks"? Arguille sees this as an opportunity to see what kind of latitude and support he is going to get from GW. Arguille had observed GW not wearing his car seat belt which was a company policy. He then looks at GW and ask," well GW. how am I suppose to support a Company Policy of wearing seat belts when the man sitting in that chair (pointing at GW) does not wear his"? Arguille could hear Paul's ass hole pucker GW put both hands behind his head, leaned back in his high back chair and said reflectively "I never did get use to wearing that son of a bitch". No wrath from GW was delivered and Arguille had determined the support he needed was in place. GW religiously wore his seat belt from that day forward You could see Paul relax both physically and emotionally with a look of surprise at the docile response from GW

Arguille was now positioned to proceed with his format to improve the overall performance of the surface facilities. Processing facility, rail line, gondola loading and river barge loading all required upgrade due to lack of attention. Previous management had blatantly ignored their responsibilities. After two months at the operation Arguille uncovered issues with management personnel having sexual relations with hourly worker wives. This was the tip of the iceberg of problems to be corrected.

Three months into the Project the hourly workers announced their annual cookout. This was open invitation but due to bad relations few in management attended in the past. In this short period Arguille had dismissed those in management that were having relations with employee spouses and it was time for fence mending. He required all management to attend the cookout. The event was scheduled for the next Saturday. The day arrived and Arguille with his General operating Foreman, Stoney, arrived around 2:00. The event had been in action since 8:00. As they approached the crowd of approximately 200 an unsettling silence fell over the group. Sensing the tension in the group Arguille approached two of the workers and offered to buy them a beer at the 4 keg refreshment stand. A smile developed on the two workers and Arguille presented the beer. This broke the ice with the workers and an air of camaraderie eventually premeditated the event. Three workers had spent the night manning the spit and charcoal fire. The charcoal was placed in a large ellipse so the drippings from the pig would not flare up and burn the entrée. A large pig with the chest cavity filled with kielbasa and sausage had reached a golden brown and was ready for serving. The aroma of the basted bovine seemed to becon the down wind passerby for sampling.

With the two long tables covered with various and extensive side dishes provided by the worker families. This was a feast fit for royalty. This spread was provided for all and was consumed with vigor by the attendees. Arguille took advantage of the situation to create an atmosphere of friendship with workers and their families. He took time to visit all the family tables at the event. Thus in the future if anyone heard the name Arguille MacGregor they would know the person. This was not the approach of previous management and had perpetuated an air of animosity. Attendees were pleased with the new approach.

Arguille and Stoney departed at 10:00 after giving parting salutations to the group and expressions of gratitude. Stoney was dropped off at his car. Still a single fellow Arguille was not yet ready to return home, over his stay in the area he had visited several of the local bars and had developed a liking for a particular three establishments. One of the three, The Yardarm, he decided to stop for a night cap. He entered the blue collar environment that was occupied by late 20s young adults. Arguille noticed a stunning blue eyed brunette that was sitting alone near the bar. He navigated through the crowd and asked the lovely lady if he could join her. Her response was subdued but positive. He sat beside her and asked her name which was Mary. He offered to buy a drink and she accepted requesting tequila. Conversing over their refreshments Arguille noticed she was wearing a short skirt and low cut net blouse that revealed an ample cleavage. Double D for sure. He speculated if he had the opportunity to place his nose there and emit a sound he would hear an echo. She was a college student in for a short weekend to visit her family.

They continued to talk for an hour and became more interested in each other as time passed. After some time Arguille took the liberty of putting his hand on her inner thigh. There was no objection on her part and she returned the action on Arguille. After a ten minute interval Mary whispered to Arguille they should leave. She also recommended they leave in her car a late model Corvette. She drove to a nearby remote state park that was deserted giving the late hour. Arguille continued to stroke her inner thy the entire time of travel. To his delight this also allowed him to determine she had no under garments.

Mary drove to one of the remote sites with State Park tables and small welcome center that was uninhabited. Arguille was not sure what was going to happen next. Mary walked over to one of the tables and motioned for Arguille to follow. He complied and as he approached Mary she brought him into her arms and gave him a hot inviting kiss. Arguille opened her knit blouse and kissed her breast which she enjoyed (no echo encountered). He then raised her skirt and undid himself as they reclined on the table in heated passion. Mary wrapped her legs around Arguille as he placed his hands under her buttocks to pull her in as tight as possible. Arguille had an instantaneous flash back to his underground mining experience when the equipment had penetrated the seam to the hotizontal limit of the equipment it was said to be "all sumped up". Arguille was definitely "all sumped up" with no complaints from Mary. They enjoyed each other as Arguille played look out for any vehicles that might appear but maintaining their passionate rhythm. None did and they satisfied each other completely for almost an hour. Arguille seldom was able to maintain an erection through multiple erections. This was one of those situations.

They lay in sweating silence catching their breath from their intense interlude. They then corrected and straightened their clothing and returned to Mary's car. Aiguilles legs were trembling. They were traveling back to Arguille's car when he asked her for a last name. She replied, "Windelkowski". **PANIC, SHE WAS GW's DAUGHTER.** Arguille tried to hide his astonishment and fear. Mary had failed to ask for his name earlier but did now and Arguille responded "Marcus Cadd" hoping to never see her or the Yardarm again.

Arguille put this episode behind him even though the sexual act had and would remain one of the most exciting of his life. Arguille had performed well on two levels. One he had not planned on but would never forget. One level was professional and the second was recreational.

SLICK

ARGUILLE CONTINUED TO develop and expand a reputation as an industrial problem-solving guru. He had gotten the attention of corporate level managers and was the GO-TO person for issue resolution. Issues associated with Safety, Performance, Human Resources, Quality Control, Financial Success and Facility Profit had all been dealt with successfully under his management and control. His expertise had developed his know how across the many different corporate and worker cultures across the U.S... Arguille attributed this success to his own personal philosophy that all issues and successes are 80% people and 20% facility. Tackle the people problems first and all else will fall in place with the assistance of exceptionally qualified personnel.

Arguille was promoted to the next operational disaster to fix. The General Managers name was Arch. A highly respected man who commanded respect just by his presence in a room. Arch was an acquaintance of Arguille and was familiar with his abilities With operational availability then at 56% (the norm was 95%) the facility was restricting throughput to the total multi billion dollar steel operation. Bottle neck was kind in the description of the magnitude of the restrictive effect. Correction of this blockage was required immediately or potential for shuttering the entire operation with 20,000 permanent layoffs was possible. After two months at the operation Arguille quantified the problem and determined the five priority issues were labor relations, maintenance hours, old technology, complacent management and corporate intervention.

With the promotion came the directive that Arguille had unlimited resources and eighteen months to show overall improvement, or he would be out of a job and the facility closed. This was not unusual for Arguille as the high level of his income came with a similar stress level. He knew of only one person with the dynamic skills required to achieve the goal. That person was "Slick" Dave.

He acquired the name "Slick" from his early employment days after graduating from Penn State in Mechanical Engineering. He had a propensity for redesigning mill processes and became known in the industry for his expertise. He enjoyed being involved in the maintenance of steel facilities that could often be dangerous if not deadly. A man of Scottish decent found himself involved with a maintenance crew on a weekend which was the only time he could gain access to an otherwise 24/7 operation. With the necessity of accessing the massive moving parts of the process it was unavoidable not to become covered in the lubricants required in the process. One of the typical operation weekends he was exiting the mechanical internals after inspecting the status of a modification. He had designed and installed the modification just installed. In the process he became incrusted in the lubricant that coated the internal walls of the device. As he exited a worker observed him appearing and exclaimed "good afternoon Slick" referring to his exterior condition, Coated with lubricant from his close-up inspections of the massive machinery. This was a sign of respect and camaraderie which followed him the rest of his days.

Arguille immediately contacted Slick to join him on a most difficult task that only Slick and Arguille understood. No lengthy conversation was required as their previous undertakings had not been for the faint of heart and Slick expected a similar circumstance now. His ten-year relationship with Arguille had been challenging, educational and financially rewarding.

Meeting at the Pittsburg Airport the two shook hands and enjoyed being together again for another high-profile work adventure. This would present risk of unknown depth and dimensions. It was a major challenge with low probability of success, but these were the two individuals most qualified to attempt the turnaround.

The origin of all work problems were 80% people and 20% equipment would surely apply here. To address these communications with the 5000 Pennsylvania workers. A plan had to be developed as those in recent times had been volatile and aggressive toward management. The two heroes scheduled one-hour meetings with 5000 workers each to open communications. The first meeting began with an audience of totally quiet members. Very unusual circumstance. The agenda consisted of a get to know your introduction then presentation of the plan to turn the facility around. This included the target of 18 months and potential facility closure if not achieved. This was received with resentment as revealed by the body English of a restrained defensive tackle in the NFL. Having listened to unrealized management promises in the past the audience of 5000 had little faith in what they were being presented. Culturally of Italian, Polish, Russian and German descent the workers were a true cross section of the States inhabitants After completing the presentation Arguille asked if there were any questions. The auditorium was silent. This was a definite litmus test of how serious the situation was.

Similar receptions were observed until the 4th of 4 meetings and finally were completed. Arguille and Slick asked the group collectively what they thought of the presentation and would they work with them. The typical silence prevailed until suddenly all eyes turned to one individual. The individual with a projected presence of a commander looked at Arguille and stated, "We will give you six months". Ah ha, Arguille and Slick had just found the true natural leader of the group. The individual had no affiliation with any union hierarchy. They had learned from experience there was always a natural leader irrespective of union official agendas that the workers respected and followed. Slick later learned the individual was a Baptist minister, highly intelligent by the name of Adam nick name of Preacher. This was the first team member of the problem solution effort.

Arguille and Slick began to identify and prioritize their battle plan to turn the facility around. Labor relations were not in the best conditions as a lack of communications and sporadic sexual activity between workers wives and supervisors. The supervisors involved were over time dismissed and eliminated from the work force over a six-month period. To improve communications Adam was brought into the planning stage which extrapolated into the hourly workers. Slick established an initiative for addressing grievances on a worker to management direct communication on issues. On every two weeks basis Slick would meet with the individual workers to discuss issues and hopefully arrive at a solution. A level of trust and commitment had to be established for the system to work. Arguille knew Slick was excellent at this effort.

Reviewing the total picture Arguille, Slick and Preacher composed a list of items to address to improve the overall economic situation of the facility. They were labor relations, quality control, and availability through mechanical maintenance, financial success and future plan.

Previous management had pursued a philosophy of *cheapest* versus *lowest cost*. The facility had been operated without communications to the work force and minimal expense on maintenance. The low availability required longer hours of operation to achieve scheduled sales volume. Slick was familiar with this scenario prompted by upper management producing above plan low cost at the expense of availability. This in an effort to receive salary bonuses based on production volume.

Slick enlisted the aid of Tom, two supervisors and four representatives from the work force. The Preacher and Slick had to have an open mind and thick skin to take the brunt of pinned up animosity and establishes fertile ground for communications. They collectively decided to hold breakfast meetings with the workforce on a volunteer basis and cover current issues. The first of the series were more a complaint session for the workers but over time developed into an honest team effort at problem resolution.

The next item into the turnaround Plan was quality control. Variability in the final product had created a fifteen percent rejection rate due to variability. The team developed a program to investigate the root causes and develop resolutions to correct. The investigation led to the discovery of three causes of variability. The storage of the final product created particle segregation due to size that created variability when inventories were low or high. A computer program was developed to maintain product inventories at stationary levels. The second cause was a bias in the product sample system due to geometry issues. An estimate to make the necessary design changes was developed and implemented. The final result would be confirmed in three months. The third quality issue was identified as variability in the feed material. Inherent quality per feed stream was found to be consistent but different ratios created corresponding variability in the product. The team had developed a system of raw material feeders that stabilized the feed quality through proper proportional blending. Slick and his Team had developed a solid solution to this one element of the turnaround.

As a standalone Profit Center, the facility had been losing money for the last 2 years. Arguille had been investigating the reasons for the loss. He arrived at three underlying reasons:

1. Product market value had dropped 20% over the period.
2. A review of supplier cost had not been actioned.
3. A review of labor cost was to be conducted.

A meeting with Slick and Adam developed a strategy to address all three. Arguille and Slick reviewed the process improvements and approached the customers to assist in their cost reductions to improve revenue rates. Recovery improvements of 10% were realized on process improvements with electronic technology improvements. Higher recoveries were realized with the upgrades.

Hourly worker cost were 10% above industry standards. Arguille, Slick and Adam quantified this and collectively developed a plan to reduce this, the hourly office workers were communicated with and a plan to reduce cost through job description consolidation stringent work hour control was implemented.

The changes were massive and a whirlwind for the workers. This was two months into the Project. The trio knew they had to maintain the trust of the crews or the plan would fail. It was time for a spring cook out for the crews that was a yearly event. This would be a litmus test for management and crews to see if all was on track. The kegs of beer, massive cover dish display and roasted kielbasa stuffed pig were all planned and in place for the *"Barbie"* were all operation by noon. A Vegan buffet was provided also to make sure all cultures and generations were covered and available.

Arguille and Slick were not certain just how they would be received but understood how important this event was to the crews. They arrived together not knowing if they would perceived as Attila The Hun and Jack the Ripper or Mr. Rogers and Smokey the Bear (Slick was rather large). They walked at a regular pace and approached the beer keg table. The group was silent. It was deafening. Understanding this was a make or break moment Arguille looked at the group and said "can I buy anyone a beer". Three workers responded they would like one so Arguille did the honors. Arguille gave an Irish toast "may you be in Heaven an hour before the devil knows you dead". They drank their first taste then the majority stepped up for their first drink. Arguille continued until he ran out if Irish toast then passed the pouring honors to Slick.

The event continued until late into the night with all with a better understanding of each other's position and appreciation for the reason for the effort. Many of the workers had not understood the gravity of the situation until this event. A much more in depth concept of requirements to successfully survive was appreciated by the workforce.

Entering the fourth month of the Program an improvement of five percentage points which was a major improvement in the scheme of things was realized This was shared with all and did spark a bit of enthusiasm that success was possible. This was to be the launching point of a major turnaround.

Reinforcing the programs that were already in place confirmed the sustainability of the initial program. Now to extend the program Supplier cost was reviewed in detail. Supplier inventory control was confirmed to be on a FIFO (First in First Out) basis with minimum inventory at any one location. This coupled with JIT (Just in Time) delivery of manufactured materials greatly reduced the cash held in inventory. The effect on profit was an increase of 8% which was the highest in 3 years. The obvious risk was any interruption in supply was a halt in production. With the risk of a plant closure it was a reasonable undertaking.

The 8th month of the effort began to see a consistent improvement in the facility. Performance in general was on a positive trend across the total facility. The final element in the program was to sustain the program. This could only be effected through continuous improvement and new technology.

Arguille, Slick, and Adam discussed the agenda for this approach. The continuous improvement was to be actioned through state legislation that benefited the facility processes and human resources. A plan to think outside the box would new technologies to include Artificial Intelligence, Robotics and 3-D Printing. A three year plan to be developed and implemented to assess these methods and applications viability. A four man team representative of the total facility to drive the effort was assembled. A one year 10% benefit in cost reduction or profit to be calculated and distributed to the employees.

After fourteen months of protracted effort the performance had increased to a much motivational level of 87%. The implementation of the program was achieving the desired effect and with the addition of the "outside the box" criteria goals would be met.

Arguille had again validated his reputation as a problem solver with the use of his two philosophies 1) First step is to define the facility problem and 2) all problems are 80% people and 20% process. He had defined and quantified the issues and developed a plan with the help of Slick. They then fired a salvo of effort over time at the issues. With the aid and support from the crews the 80% of the issues brought the result to the required success.

HUEY

ARGUILLE FOUND HIMSELF with time on his hands in the autumn of the year. Work had been a continuous six days a week and with a weeklong facility maintenance outage scheduled he decided to make some impromptu visits. The weather was dry and the hardwood trees display of fall leaves was too inviting to pass up. Arguille would pack his tent and camping gear. He would then escape to the mountain ridges of West Virginia, Kentucky and Pennsylvania. The brilliant orange, red and yellow leaves of the trees were again a divine mosaic that only lasted two weeks. Once the fall rains arrived the awesome foliage would disappear to the earth and create nourishment for the next year presentation. From sunrise to sunset Arguille would travel in his leased all terrain vehicle and occasionally take a friend.

This year he had invited a high school buddy, Jerry James with a nick name of G.I. to travel with him. GI had been a running back at the University of Kentucky He was a health advocate that enjoyed the outdoors and was also a "black powder" fire arm enthusiast as was Arguille. This sport allowing only one shot for a successful dear kill.

The early morning weather was cool and dry. Fall rains had not yet arrived so hunting conditions were excellent. The first two days hunting indicating many signs of bucks but none were within rage.

The third day of the one week season the two outdoorsman were up before dawn and located themselves in strategic locations to observe an unfortunate trophy.

Just at the boundary between daylight and dark a hapless eight point buck happened to appear well camouflaged in the trees within the range of Arguille. He already has his rifle elevated, sighted the animal, took a deep breath and fired his weapon. The recoil from the shot jolted Arguille which he had prepared for.. The buck instantaneously began to vault but the aim had been accurate and true. The buck fell to the ground.

Arguille moved rapidly to the fallen trophy and met GI at roughly the same time after hearing the shot. GI exclaimed ("well done") and shook the hand of Arguille. Before beginning to field dress the buck. The hunters confirmed the eyes were open confirming the kill. Closed eyes indicated the animal was still alive and could be extremely dangerous. Confirming the eyes were open and the animal was no longer alive. GI began the field dressing at a physical location the buck would not have appreciated.as the testicles were first to be removed.

With the prize transported and loaded in their vehicle the two adventures broke their camp, loaded their gear and headed for the nearest game check in and taxidermist. They bartered with the taxidermist to trade the meat of the deer for a mounting of the head. The proprietor agreed to the trade as the hunters had no need for the carcass and the proprietor had a large family

Exiting the taxidermist shop they realized they had three more days of time off so they decided to take advantage of them. Leaving from Bluefield, Virginia they set their sights on Lexington, Kentucky, and horse racing.

Striking out for Lexington the four hour drive was temporarily picturesque. The fall rains had begun and the beautiful foliage on the hard woods would soon be gone. The weather had been kind to allow the dense foliage for the camouflage tracking of their prize buck. Arguille contacted his friend Huey that he was in town and asked if they could meet at the local track tomorrow. Huey responded he was happy to see Arguille was in town and would be pleased to meet Huey around noon at the track.

Arguille and GI arrived at the track parking lot at noon and began the walk to the dirt track entrance. High with anticipation of a second sporting win after the trophy buck. They paid the entrance fee, collected a fact sheet and race schedule for the afternoon. Proceeding on into the stands GI noticed another acquaintance sitting nearby. It was Marcus, a gay millionaire, that had acquired his fortune from the coal industry. The other was Huey, a local well known chemical salesman. Huey had just arrived also but Marcus had been there for over two hours. Marcus had extraordinary luck that day and had not lost a race the entire time. Loose money was protruding from Marcus pockets as evidence of his success. He had been drinking most of the day and was well relaxed at the moment.

Marcus and Huey got into a conversation while Arguille and GI listened concerning Marcus new Escalade and the money he had accumulated.. Huey fell in love with the Escalade he had spotted in the parking lot. All four of the gang carried on a conversation while enjoying a drink. Marcus relayed to Huey he had not lost at betting on a race the entire day. He had bundles of cash protruding from his pants, shirt and jacket were all filled with cash to capacity. This being a confirmation of his success. He then asked Huey how much money he was carrying and Huey responded "$200". Marcus told Huey to put the entire amount on #4, Lucky Louis, to win. Huey told Marcus this was his last $200 and he could not afford to lose it. Marcus replied not to worry if #4 did not win he would give Huey his Escalaide. Huey left the group and returned with ticket in hand for the race and great anticipation for the race to begin.

After what seemed to be an eternity the bugler announced "CALL TO POST " to escort the thoroughbreds to the starting gate. Once located back with the group Huey settled back with his drink, ticket in hand and view of the 1.2 mile oval track. All ten thoroughbreds were lined up at the starting gate and anxiously waiting for the start. The trainers worked feverously to get the animals to settle. Emanating from the starting gate the words, "ON YOUR MARK, GET SET, BANG" went the starting pistol and all ten thoroughbreds leapt to the start. The first turn complete #4 was mid way of the pack. On they charged with each stride throwing soil high into the air with the power of each hoof striking the track. As they approached the second turn #4 was in great command of the next to last position. Huey was starting to get concerned as his $200 pick had done nothing but lose ground

Good ole #4 was now in last place with a great vision of the derrieres of the contestant directly in front of him, the horse and the jockey. The rhythmic stride of the horse directly in front of #4 just happened to be named "Ash a Nine" and was an omen Huey and Marcus had over looked. Huey was getting furious as his last $200 was disappearing in front of his eyes. As the finish line slowly appeared on the horizon #4 was six links (48 feet) behind the behind to his front and Lucky Louie came in dead last.

Huey was livid at the race finish. He turned to his gay millionaire friend and unloaded his verbal displeasure at length. He told Marcus he could run faster than Huey finished his tirade by stating he could run faster than Lucky Louie. Seizing on the moment and the stress of Huey, Marcus turned to him and offered if he would run one loop of the track he would give Huey his Escalade!! Huey was astonished! Regaining composure Huey saw the sincerity in his friend's eyes and immediately bolted down the steps and onto the track. Removing his shoes and socks with a speed superman would be proud of Huey assumed a 3 point stance and began his run. A man in his 40's Huey had no problem with the first ½ of the track. Since Huey was well recognized around Lexington the people in the stands began to shout in unison, "GO HUEY, GO HUEY, GO HUEY". Huey could hear the shouts of support from the throng of attendees which greatly motivated him. Rounding the second turn Huey could feel his heart pounding along with the sweat he had developed and legs that felt like tree stumps. To his dismay he could see the finish line but also a Police car with light flashing across the track. He slowed to a trot and approached the Police car with Officer. The Officer was also an acquaintance off Huey and had a light hearted attitude of the event he had just witnessed.

The officer explained to Huey he had broken the Law and he was required to take him to the station and book him on a misdemeanor charge. As the officer handcuffed Huey there was little resistance between gasping for air and not being a stranger to the feel of the cuffs. Arguille, Marcus and GI watched the events unfold from the stands. They followed the police car to the station in the Escalade and after posting $200 in bond (Huey was penny less) they retrieved Huey from the station. Huey was in good humor as the episode had been one to remember for a lifetime. He had also retrieved his socks and shoes at the station. They all finished the day over dinner Marcus covering the cost. The next morning Arguille and GI headed east to return home. Marcus had breakfast of country ham, biscuits and gravy, fried potatoes and fried apples on his estate veranda. Huey awoke to a bright morning sun light and peering outside to see the new Escalade outside his apartment. The keys and title were inside as Marcus had promised. Arguille's faith was once again affirmed in the human spirit.

ARGUILLE THE LIFE SAVER

ARGUILLE WAS TAKING a moment to reflect on his many faceted lives at *"Babes"* Restaurant prior to work time. Locate in southern West Virginia *Babes* was famous for their Western omelets and the sausage, peppers, potatoes, onions and cheese that made up the basic ingredients. For additional flavoring he would always ask for two anchovies to be added to the four egg masterpiece. This had been designated by the workers as "The Arguille Special". This was a good start for the day when topped off with the house specialty of black Colombian coffee.

Getting in position in his company supplied vehicle Arguille strapped himself in and started the last ten mile drive to the operation. While driving he reflected on the plan for the day which included loading from a concrete silo to fill two-10,000 ton gondola unit trains for export to France. The material to be loaded had been formed over the last two hundred thousand years and contained methane gas between the horizontal laminations of the seam. Large volumes of air were mechanically pulled through the underground operation to keep the percentage methane below 5% the explosive range of the mixture. Weather had been forecast as a low pressure front moving through the area. This would effect the release of methane directly as the lower the barometric pressure the higher the volume of methane was released. The operation was a 24 hour per day facility and had operated the entire night with no interruptions to operations. He greeted the oncoming crew and went to his office for a summary of the previous shift report.

With the focus on safety this was the first topic reviewed at each shift. No accidents, injuries or events were reported. Elevated levels of methane had been reported in some areas but none that exceeded 2%. Product quality and volume all met requirements and were satisfactory. The loading of the first unit train from the product concrete silo had begun. Arguille began his customary walk through the facility as was his usual morning ritual. Due to his short time allowed he had trained himself to observe any changes or out of the ordinary conditions to report to operations for further investigation. As he rapidly walked through the nine floors of the facility he noticed the exhaust fan on the top of product silo. This was a negative draft tubular device which pulled fresh air across the top inside of the silo diluting any accumulated methane. The motor and fan resided inside the 3 foot diameter metal fan tube and were driven a single belt. The discharge from fan usually took the shape resembling that of the exhaust from a jet fighter. Not so the tube exit today. In the early morning moisture the exhaust trail had no evidence of any force and slowly languished from the end of the tube. This alerted Arguille to a change in condition and with the anticipated increase in methane liberation was cause for alarm. Arguille completed his plant inspection through all nine floors. He then left for the top of the 10,000 ton silo to the location of the exhaust fan. Once there somewhat breathless he opened the inspection fan. Inside he saw 2 seized bolts holding the bearing on the fan shaft, a broken drive belt and a fan shaft that was not turning. There was no ventilation air going through the silo. Arguille contacted the plant maintenance superintendent and explained the situation. The superintendent said he would dispatch a 3 man crew with replacement bolts and new belt for the fan drive to include a oxygen-acetylene torch to remove the failed bolts.

Arguille waited for 10 minutes until the crew was on their way. He left the top of the silo and while walking down the singular walkway exit passed the repair crew on the way to the fan. A device used for measuring methane is an approved hand held device referred to as an anemometer or "spotter". This device would measure methane levels up to 15%. While Arguille proceeded on to the office he was thinking of the repair to take place. The failed bolt would have to be removed the failed bolt with the oxy-act flame torch and replaced. He then realized he had not seen a spotter for a pre burn methane level check carried by the crew. A flame inside the fan tube could cause a catastrophic explosion upon ignition of the mixture. Arguille had given his radio to the newly arrived crew and had no communications. He immediately began running back up the walkway to the top of the silo for fear the workers would ignite the internal containment of the silo by ignited torch with no methane check. The horizontal discharge tube could contain methane in the explosive range if present and internal of the silo..

Arguille arrived to the silo top and observed one worker on one knee with an oxygen/acetylene torch in hand preparing to ignite the flame torch. Arguille screamed for the worker to stop. With a puzzled look the worker waited for instruction. Arguille handed the worker his spotter and asked him to take a reading. The worker extended his hand through the observation port with the spotter and pressed the read button of the spotter. The electronic display read 5.85% methane well within the explosive range of the atmosphere. If the open flame of the torch had been ignited an explosion would have followed and 4 lives lost.

If Arguille had not ran up the walkway he would not have reached the site in time to avert a catastrophe. The entire crew was appreciative of the actions by Arguille. Arguille gratified that his years of a multifaceted experience had given him the skills to be an expert leader.

GOOD BYE

The next episode for Arguille occurred when a supervisor came in his office and informed Arguille the afternoon crew was not in the prep room for the evening shift at 3:00. It was 2:30. Instead of alerting HR to the situation Arguille drove 2 miles from the office where he found the evening shift crew parked off the side of the road. Not knowing the attitude of the workers Arguille exited his vehicle with great apprehension. Stepping in front of the crew of 40 Arguille stated "OK fellows, what is the issue"? The response was that they were going to be replaced by Hispanic migrant workers at a lower wage scale. One of the workers had gone through the office and overheard a piece of a conversation relating to migrant workers but in no relation to the facility. He assured the crew there were no considerations on the use of migrant workers at this time. Arguille did inform them if they did not begin work at 3:00 this action would be considered an unauthorized work stoppage. They would all be disciplined and any resolution would be out of his hands and control. Recognizing how serious the situation could become the workers moved toward their vehicles without hesitation. To avoid a confrontation and negative outcome for all Arguille noticed his watch read 3:00 for 10 continuous minutes. This gained Arguille a great deal of respect with the workers and paid him worker relation dividends for his entire stay at this facility.

Arguille also realized that most worker issues were personal complaints and not related to any violation to the Contractual Agreement. Based on this Arguille would ask which part of the agreement had been violated in a grievance meeting. Nine times out of ten the worker with the issue could not identify any part of the agreement only personal complaints about a supervisor or other worker but not the Agreement. This reduced the number of issues that went to HR by 80%. A new low level of complaint activity had been achieved and in doing so a marked improvement in performance was reached.

Arguille was unsure if he had made any lasting relationship with the workers. He had been promoted to another troubled facility the operation. and would be leaving. While finishing his last day at the facility one of the workers came to his office and requested he meet the afternoon shift at the prep room prior to start time. With apprehension he entered the room. The entire crew stood at attention as Arguille entered the room. Argüelles had no idea why the gathering. One worker approached him and presented him with a small box. Arguille accepted the box, opened it and to his amazement retrieved a solid gold railroad pocket watch. Inside the watch was an engraving that read "Thanks From 2nd Shift Crew". Arguille knew of no similar presentation in the entire industry, In spite of his best effort a singular tear streaked slowly down his check. He tried to say a few words but the words stuck in his throat. The Crew understood.

Humanity understands sincerity.

REFLECTION

Arguille had achieved his many goals in life and bucket list items and was considering the final arc section in his Circle of Life. Not knowing if he would leave the earth in a final adventure or simply pass in the night (or day). Whichever the Almighty had ordained, he was content with his accomplishments and had left instructions to be cremated upon his passing. This relieving the financial burden on the family with burial expenses and allowing the earliest possible continuance of the travel of the dust to dust Circle of Life outcome. His Divinely guided Drake Equation ... outcome and return to the cosmos with life maintaining cosmic dust it contained. ∞